THE LEGACY SERIES

SERIES TITLES

How We Do Things Here
Matt Cashion

Neon Steel
Jennifer Maritza McCauley

Release of Information
Kali White VanBaale

The Divide
Evan Morgan Williams

Yes, No, I Don't Know
Kathryn Gahl

The Price of Their Toys
John Loonam

The Caged Man
Calvin Mills

A Day Doesn't Go By When I Don't Have Regrets
J. Malcolm Garcia

These Are My People
Steve Fox

We Should Be Somewhere by Now
Stephen Tuttle

Burner and Other Stories
Katrina Denza

The Plan of Chicago
Barry Pearce

Trust Issues
K.P. Davis

Adult Children
Laurence Klavan

Guardians & Saints
Diane Josefowicz

Western Terminus: Stories and A Novella
Michael Keefe

Like Human
Janet Goldberg

The Hopefuls
Elizabeth Oness

Never Stop Exiting
Michael Hopkins

Broken Heart Syndrome
Anne Colwell

The Mexican Messiah: A Novella & Stories
Jay Kauffmann

Close to a Flame
Colleen Alles

American Animism
Jamey Gallagher

Keeping What's Best Left Kept Secret
David Ricchiute

Soaked
Toby LeBlanc

The Path of Totality
Marie Zhuikov

Shocker in Gloomtown
Dan Libman

The Continental Divide
Bob Johnson

The Three Devils and Other Stories
William Luvaas

The Correct Response
Manfred Gabriel

Welcome Back to the World: A Novella & Stories
Rob Davidson

Greyhound Cowboy and Other Stories
Ken Post

Close Call
Kim Suhr

The Waterman
Gary Schanbacher

Signs of the Imminent Apocalypse and Other Stories
Heidi Bell

What We Might Become
Sara Reish Desmond

The Silver State Stories
Michael Darcher

An Instinct for Movement
Michael Mattes

The Machine We Trust
Tim Conrad

Gridlock
Brett Biebel

Salt Folk
Ryan Habermeyer

The Commission of Inquiry
Patrick Nevins

Maximum Speed
Kevin Clouther

Reach Her in This Light
Jane Curtis

The Spirit in My Shoes
John Michael Cummings

*The Effects of Urban Renewal on Mid-Century America and
Other Crime Stories*
Jeff Esterholm

What Makes You Think You're Supposed to Feel Better
Jody Hobbs Hesler

Fugitive Daydreams
Leah McCormack

Readers will revel in the fragile, fragmented lives of Cashion's characters, each of whom ripples outward toward one another, creating a strange convergence of community in their overlapping lives. These are people who've plied themselves from the page, people whose breath we feel in every line, with humor and heartache to boot. Matt Cashion is the Elizabeth Strout of the Midwest, revealing the thrumming heartbeat of lives equally mundane and miraculous—but wondrously mortal most of all.

—BJ HOLLARS
author of *Year of Plenty*

I've been reading Matt Cashion's dazzling fiction now for over thirty years and marveling at every chiseled sentence he commits to the page. It is no exaggeration to passionately declare that *How We Do Things Here* is his best book to date. Cashion is an absolute master of short fiction; he channels, by turns, Andre Dubus and Richard Ford and leavens it all with lightning strikes of Flannery O'Connor—tight-lipped laser precision, domesticity elevated to wry opera, wildly imaginative diction, unmatched wit, often sheer hilarity. These stories are indisputably terrific. What a thrill to read *How We Do Things Here* and witness Matt Cashion get better and better—if that's even possible—sentence by sentence, page by page, before our very eyes.

—JOSEPH BATHANTI
author of *Too Glorious to Even Long for on Certain Days*

How We Do Things Here is a tapestry of vibrant stories woven with keen insights, quirky revelations, and witty intellect. Humor sewn throughout. Spanning Wisconsin to Florida, this emotionally binding collection is adorned with compassion and zest. Readers are awed with the propulsive spin Cashion uses to deftly weave these tales. Even in the midst of sad, incomprehensible absurdity (isn't there so much of that these days?) we see there's still so much to relish and value: a close relationship, a startling memory, a therapeutic laugh.

—KEITH PILAPIL LESMEISTER
author of *We Could've Been Happy Here*

How We Do Things Here

stories

Matt Cashion

CORNERSTONE PRESS

UNIVERSITY OF WISCONSIN-STEVENS POINT

Cornerstone Press, Stevens Point, Wisconsin 54481
Copyright © 2026 Matt Cashion
www.uwsp.edu/cornerstone

Printed in the United States of America.

Library of Congress Control Number: 2026931110
ISBN: 978-1-968148-22-5

Cornerstone Press titles are produced in courses and internships offered by the Department of English at the University of Wisconsin–Stevens Point.

*for Heather,
again, still, evermore*

How We Do Things Here

I didn't like the looks of our new neighbor or the fact that he was standing in the middle of *my* backyard (framed in my U-Haul's rearview mirror) holding two beers while I maneuvered from the alley, waving with his free arm for me to keep coming, keep coming, then a closed fist sign for stop. I didn't like his buzz cut and big sunglasses, his stoic face, blank as a cinderblock, his khaki shorts with hiking boots, or the pistol on his hip, jutting out like an appendage. I wanted to drive back to Florida. But I'd made the trip for Maria, and I could hear her in my head saying *don't be an asshole for once; give it a chance.* Then his wife and two teenage kids came marching into the yard, wearing gloves, eager to help us unload. It made me suspicious. When I hit the ground, he handed me a beer and when Maria stepped up (after parking the car and unloading the cats), he handed her the other.

"Welcome to Wisconsin," he said. "This is how we do things here. Name's Karl. That's Kim, Cody, and Katy."

I looked at Maria, who looked at Kim, a serious woman on a mission, already raising the U-Haul door, ordering her silent kids to grab things and take them where Maria told them to. Maria winked at me and turned up her beer and Karl said, "'Atta girl."

It was 8 p.m., early August, still light, much milder than the Florida air we'd left two days earlier. We worried—even before seeing Karl—that we were moving toward a mistake, that we wouldn't fit in, that winter would kill us, that we shouldn't have bought a fixer-upper built in 1881 in a marginal neighborhood with such small yards that every passerby would have to say hello. But it's what we could afford on one salary (Maria's), and I made promises about becoming a handyman, which I imagined liking because I would work alone. I preferred life with headphones, hoarded privacy, subscribed to the good fences make good neighbors rule. Maria was kinder, outgoing. She *liked* having friends. She said my selfishness would cost me a spouse one day, said if I was joining her on this journey I'd have to change, learn to be a selfless partner and compassionate human, so I'd said yes, sure, of course, fearing life without her, and I promised the new me was underway.

I handed my beer back to Karl. "I'm recovering," I said. I hoped he'd see me as a veteran of wild times, loaded with stories. I'd decided to swear it off for good this time, try the fresh start in a new place routine, hoped my sobriety would be a big part of the new me.

"He's allergic to alcohol," said Maria, the truth-teller. When I turned thirty-five, every kind of alcohol made me sick, despite my exhaustive efforts to find something that didn't.

Karl's face stayed blank. I think I'd broken his heart.

"Oh," he said. "Okay. No problem." Those hard and sustained *O*'s were signs of a new and interesting territory.

He said, "Sounds like you guys got a bit of a accent." Then he jumped to work, lifting three boxes at once until the boxes were gone and *he* directed *me* (with too much energy for my taste) to grab the ends of couches and mattresses, dressers, tables, Maria's piano, and in an hour the truck was empty and I was sweating (he wasn't) and Kim said goodnight and followed her gloomy children home, just like that. I hoped Karl would leave too—we were tired—but he stopped at the cooler on his back stoop and returned with new beers for himself and Maria, then sat on the ground, back against our house, which meant we sat too, facing an orange streak of sinking light. We told him Maria's new job as a music professor had brought us here, how I'd quit a nursing job to be a househusband. We had no kids and couldn't imagine having any. I doubted then, as Maria also doubted, that I'd ever be mature enough to be a parent.

"He got fired," Maria said, but she was laughing. She knew I'd helped a terminal patient die without the required signatures, and she had admired me for it.

"Househusband?" Karl said, skipping over Maria's job and my firing. "Must be nice," he said, and seemed to mean it. He talked of being a firefighter and EMT going on twenty years, which was wearing on him, he said, hard on his marriage too because he slept at the station more than he slept at home. His sunglasses were off now, making visible the dark edges around his eyes and some deep weariness bordering on madness that made me want to keep my distance.

"It's a good neighborhood," he said.

Why the gun? I wanted to ask.

"Why the gun?" Maria asked, and *pointed*, thumb cocked, loading up for a debate.

"I wear it so I won't have to use it. It's a good neighborhood. Matter-a-fact, this Saturday is neighbor-helping-neighbor-day. We spend the day helping each other do whatever needs doing. Last year, we installed new shingles for Elvis." He pointed to the house on our other side.

All day? I thought. A *Saturday?*

"Elvis lives there?" Maria said. "Fascinating."

Roofing? In the summer?

"He's ninety-five," Karl said. "You'll hear him early in the morning; he won an impersonation contest two years ago. Last summer, he fell off a ladder and broke both legs, so I carried him to my truck and laid him in the bed and drove him to the ER and he sang the whole way there, damn fool. Said he'd survived worse. You guys like venison? I've got a freezer full."

"We're vegetarians," I said, too abruptly, hoping to sharpen the distinction between us and deter him from inviting me to go hunting.

"Not always," Maria said. She winked at me, knowing my secret. The smell of the slow-cooked barbecue at a roadside stand *begged* me to grab a sandwich I'd eat on the way home to my veggies. She must've smelled it on me. Or read the deceit on my face. She had a great nose. And great ears. All of her senses, especially her bullshit-detector, were highly refined, which was why I fell in love with her seven years ago when, after getting fired as a nurse, I worked at a piano shop and helped move a piano into her house. I loved her energetic gestures, loved how sincerely she kept apologizing for asking us to carry the piano to three rooms so she could test the acoustics, loved the music she played (though I'd never liked classical), her full bookcases, how she handed my coworker and me cans of flavored water while holding eye contact long enough to read my life without judgement, loved her wise eyes, her gentle voice. I asked for piano lessons. Did I own a piano? No. Had I *ever* played? A little in high school, on a plastic Casio. We spent my first lesson with my thumb on middle C, then I told her about being fired as a nurse—the whole story of the young woman I'd killed whose family insisted on her suffering—and surprised myself by crying. She put her hand over mine. We talked of death. We talked of parents and friends and what we wanted from our own brief lives. She said I *must* cultivate my ambition to help people, and I said, yeah, sure, without believing it. She fired me as a student (after three months), then invited me to move in. I promised to go vegetarian. I promised to stop drinking (and vomiting). I promised to read the books she gave me and to talk about them, which would help me learn selflessness. With all matters involving change, she led the way, and I tried to follow. I knew she was too good for me. I mean that her goodness was beyond my capacity for goodness, and I knew the clock was ticking on how much longer she'd wait for me to catch up.

"Vegetarians," Karl said. He scratched his chin, thinking this over.

I stood and yawned, the obvious and universal sign for *goodnight*.

"Be right back," Karl said. He walked across our yard and opened a gate in the middle of the chain-link fence we shared, then entered his garage. I hadn't noticed the gate. Turns out he and the previous owner had been best buds, so they installed the gate for easy access to each other's houses and garages.

"We'll need a new fence," I said.

"He's okay," Maria said. "He saves lives. Maybe he'll save ours one day."

Was she saying that she found him attractive? A manly man more manly than I who should be admired for qualities I did not possess, namely being nice? It sounded like an insecure position so I feared raising the question. I said, "I bet he votes for idiots. And that gun?" I reminded her that if there's a gun in the first act, it goes off in the second, just like what's-her-name claimed, and Maria said don't be dramatic, and I said don't be naive, and she said his name is Chekhov, and I said there's something strange about his wife and kids, and she said I was being a paranoid asshole and maybe I shouldn't bother unpacking, so I said nothing more.

Karl came back carrying a fishing net and a fire extinguisher. "Your housewarming gifts," he said. "The net is for *inside* bats—catch and release. Keep 'em alive to help with the mosquito problem. Or put a glove on and pluck them off the walls when they're sleeping."

"Mosquito problem?" I said.

Did Wisconsin have more mosquitoes than Florida?

"*Inside* bats?" Maria said.

"And a ghost," Karl said. "Allegedly." He extracted his phone, asked for our numbers and called them. "Save my number. I'll be your first responder."

"That's nice," Maria said, friendlier than necessary, I thought, maybe on the verge of asking him to stay longer, maybe come inside. The alley light flickered on then, orange sky dimming behind it. Two clumsy-looking bats swooped around the light.

"That thing about the ghost?" I said.

"See you Saturday," he said. "Before then too." He walked through the gate in our fence and we walked inside. Maria went straight for the pallet she'd already prepared, talking of nice neighbors and a good neighborhood, and I carried the fishing net through every room and into the basement, talking to myself of bats and ghosts, cursing our luck.

At 5 a.m., Elvis, his music, his cigarette smoke, and his barking dog woke us. He sat on his stoop and coughed and hacked and blew smoke into our open kitchen window, ten feet away. From his boombox, the real Elvis belted out "Viva Las Vegas." All morning, his dog barked at cars and people passing on our busy street. All morning, the real Elvis filled our house. Sometimes, at the end of a CD, we heard his toilet flush, then heard him moan, then sing the opening of "Heartbreak Hotel," repeating the first line only: *Since my baby left me*.

"How long before he dies?" I said, unpacking silverware.

"He's cute," Maria said. "Go introduce yourself. Be nice. Don't be yourself."

At noon, I introduced myself across our fence, learned he was nearly deaf, wore no hearing aids, and didn't think to turn down Elvis even as he kept asking me to repeat myself.

He wore a blue work shirt with "Elvis" sewn into the name patch over a breast pocket, his long sideburns were white, he was bald, frail, hunched. He bragged of what he'd survived: smallpox, an abusive father, Guadalcanal, four ex-wives, two dead children, a heart attack, a stroke, forty years working at a brewery, and three previous dogs, each named Gladys, after Elvis's mother.

"Watch out for old lady Lang," he said. "She's a mean ghost."

"Sure," I said. "Okay."

"Her husband locked her in the bedroom closet and starved her to death in 1929 is what I heard. People said they could hear her screaming, but nobody came to help. A goddamned shame is what that is. What kind of people wouldn't come running if they heard a neighbor screaming?"

"Good question," I said. "See you later."

That night at 11 p.m., I stole his boombox from his stoop and put it in my trashcan. Being deaf is one thing, being an asshole is something else. How about some consideration for the *good*-of-hearing? I did *not* (despite a passing thought) kill Gladys, who barked at every sound coming from the street our real estate agent swore was quiet, never mentioning the busses, the tractor-trailers, the farting airbrakes, the constant stream of motorcycles and dual-muffler-big trucks that Maria named our small-penis parade.

An hour later, in bed, I told Maria what I'd done, thinking she'd appreciate my efforts to secure a more peaceful neighborhood, that she might even find it amusing.

"We've made a mistake," she said, unamused.

I thought she meant that she wanted to return to Florida, to our dead-end quiet street with bigger yards and trees. What I should've said: "Moving *is* stressful."

I said, "But this is what you *wanted*."

"Maybe you should go back home," she said. "What was I thinking to believe you could get along with people? You can't change. You're incapable of growing up. You're a child."

"Am not," I said.

She picked up her phone. I imagined her Googling "Divorce lawyers near me."

A shadow moved across the ceiling and Maria screamed. It's the wingspan that's scary. Their clumsy way of knuckle-balling toward your head until the last split-second, when they veer. I watched in awe as it navigated the room, circling our bed. I wasn't sure what to do.

"Get the net," Maria said from beneath the covers.

Right. I would get the net and be a hero.

I ran down to the basement and back up to the bedroom with the net.

"Don't hurt it," Maria said.

I got frustrated with its skill of dodging the net I held up, hoping it'd fly right into it, so I started swinging. Hard. Hit it with the aluminum side. Killed it. Who knew they were so fragile?

"Did you hurt it?" Maria said.

"It's okay," said the desperate liar in me. I scooped it with the net and carried it outside. It was tangled, and I didn't want to touch it, so I got the scissors and cut around it while holding it over the trash can. It took us awhile to get to sleep.

"You have to find out how it got in," Maria said. "Plug the holes."

"No problem," I said, happy to have a job that would keep me there.

An eerie sound came from the closet like someone sliding clothes hangers.

"What's that?" Maria said.

I should've said, *Weird. Let me take a look.*

I said, "What's what?"

"We're not going to make it," she said, and turned off her lamp.

Saturday morning, still in bed, I said, "Let's take a road trip."

"Can't," she said. "It's neighbor-helping-neighbor day." She took convincing. I said we had only a few weekends before she started her new job and we deserved to reward ourselves after the stress of moving, that we'd have plenty of chances to help the neighbors, that we shouldn't feel manipulated into giving up our Saturday.

"Let's go to the Dells," I said. "We'll get Karl a gift."

We went to the Dells, the waterpark/shopping complex we'd passed on the interstate, an hour away. Bad idea. The summer was waning on everyone, so big families of screaming kids packed the place. We didn't like screaming kids. We didn't like non-screaming kids either. I bought a book called *Wisconsin Death Trip*, a nonfiction account full of photos detailing an insanity plague that hit the Black River Falls area in the late 1800s when harsh winters, scarce food, poverty, and disease created a suicide epidemic. We sat on a bench with ice cream and looked around at the sea of white people descended from the people in the book, blonde and Nordic, more white people in one place than we'd ever seen, strangely aloof-acting, distant. A couple walked by speaking German. I pointed to a sign across the street: *Torture Museum*.

She took my book, told me to enjoy myself.

I gave ten dollars to an elderly man with a bad neck who made no eye contact and offered no chit-chat. "Plus tax," he said. I gave him two more dollars, wondered if he'd still be alive when I came back out. I walked through some musty-smelling dark rooms displaying *Historic Torture Devices*: the Meatpacker's Hook, the Mouth Opener & Tongue Tearer, the Brazen Bull (a bull-shaped oven where prisoner's screams came through iron nostrils), the Head Crusher, the Judas Cradle, the Heretic's Fork, the Ducking

Stool (to "tame the shrew; a temperamental woman strapped in a chair for repeated ducking into a pond, river, cesspool, or village well"), Thumbscrews, the Bell Collar, the Gibbet ("a hanging cage for rotting corpses"), the Rake, the Rack, the Lead Sprinkler ("like a Holy Water Sprinkler filled with molten lead, hot tar, or boiling water"), the Iron Maiden of Nuremberg (a cabinet with internal spikes victims stood inside while someone slowly closed the door). There were framed photos of Death by Beast, Burning, Crucifixion, Whipping, Boiling, Starvation ("A slow and inexpensive method still used today"). I passed a seven-foot clown statue with bad teeth and entered a room devoted to Jeffrey Dahmer, John Wayne Gacy, Ed Gein, and Richard Speck "Murderabilia," featuring "Gacy's Playthings" (*adults only please*), Serial Killer Bubblegum Trading Cards, photos of corpses plastering an entire wall. And then a *Special Added Attraction*: The Three Stooges. Posters signed by Larry, Moe, and Curly, a framed letter from Shemp Howard. Beside the exit, the last photo held a man (the young owner?) gripping hands with Ronald McDonald. I looked around to say thanks, but I couldn't find him. I wondered what kind of man devotes himself to curating a torture museum. I admired him for having no boss. Did his wife (if he had one) help him dust the devices? Would his children (if he had any) fight over inheriting The Brazen Bull, The Iron Maiden? I exited to a strange shade of light, a newly-filtered world, saw Maria still on her bench reading *Wisconsin Death Trip* amidst passing tourists, a cheesy pop song blaring from corner speakers.

"Have you had enough?" she said.

"I'm ready to go home," I said.

Late Sunday afternoon, we sat at our kitchen island eating zucchini noodles covered in pesto with pine nuts, cigar smoke coming through our kitchen window. Also, a grill. With meat on it. Delicious-smelling meat that poked a nerve in my brainpan.

"Disgusting," Maria said.

"Terrible," I said.

Karl materialized outside our kitchen window, facing us, cigar in mouth, sunglasses on, four-day growth of beard. He scared us.

"Hi guys," he said. "Mind if I smoke?"

I knew Maria resented the use of *guys*. "Y'all" would've been nicer, but such language was endangered now.

"We missed you yesterday," he said.

"We took a quick trip to the Dells before Maria's school year started," I said, and felt her staring at me harshly, as if I was blaming her.

He pointed his tongs behind him, said, "I replaced that pane in your garage window that had a hole in it. I had an extra sheet of glass, so I just cut a square to fit and caulked it. You know that theory of how a hole in one window makes the neighborhood disintegrate?"

"Right," I said. I'd heard the theory—heard it from Maria, in fact—but I didn't remember there being a hole in my garage window. "Thanks," I said.

"I also fixed your garage door. Saw it wasn't closing snug. I'll show you how you can adjust the tension on the automatic opener."

Maria had noticed the gap a few days earlier, big enough for animals and burglars to crawl through, but I'd said it wasn't a big deal, meaning I didn't know how to fix it.

"I was about to fix that," I said.

The cigar and the meat were making Maria sick, something she'd say as soon as he stepped away, which I knew she was ready for him to do because she wasn't saying anything.

"I've had my garage broken into three times," he said. "They've clipped my padlocks and they've used a ladder to climb through the second floor window. I fixed your dishwasher too. Sam said it was leaking, so I replaced the washers and tightened the clamps. Hey, I got tickets for tonight's Bulls game, our semi-pro baseball team. They're not good, but they're fun to watch. Go with?"

It took a second to catch up to his invitation. I was still wondering how he'd managed to get into our house to fix the dishwasher. But no, I had no interest in sports—playing or watching—which was one thing Maria liked about me, how rare it was for a man to dislike the infantile chasing of balls and cheering of concussions.

"I should unpack some boxes," I said.

"This fall, I'll take you to a Packers game. My father left me his season tickets in his will, forty-yard-line, which I'll pass on to my kids—keep it in the family, you know."

"Sign me up," I said. We had nothing in common.

"This winter," he said. "I'll take you ice-fishing."

I didn't mean to laugh, but that's reflex for you. I imagined staring down a hole we'd cut into the ice, frozen in place for hours, maybe days.

"Count me in," I said.

"See you soon," he said. He blew smoke through our window and vanished.

"I'm changing the locks," I said.

"He's lonely," she said. "You should do something with him. Make a friend. Give your imaginary friends a break."

"They'd be jealous," I said.

The next day, while Maria worked on campus, preparing for the semester, I went to the hardware store for a new deadbolt. Here was my shot at being a handyman. I watched YouTube videos on deadbolt installation from men who were very proud of themselves. Then I called a guy who changed the locks and added a deadbolt while I went to the finished basement to unpack my 7.2 surround-sound stereo system (seven speakers, two subwoofers) and large screen TV, which I intended to spend much time with.

Then I behaved very badly. One morning in early September, I slept until 9 a.m. while Maria went for her ten-mile morning run, and while I made coffee—working around our three hungry cats (Clementine, Belvidere, and Bug Eyes)—I looked through the open window and saw Karl's child, Cody, sixteen, zooming down the alley on his skateboard, watched him sail over a ramp and vanish behind our garage, heard him crash, heard him scream. And I didn't move. My coffee wasn't ready. He kept screaming. The cats scampered. His parents weren't home. They parked in the alley; both cars were gone. His older sister wasn't home either, apparently. Or she, like me, wasn't responding. Karl spent many nights at the fire station, and Kim was rarely home; we weren't sure how she spent her time. We often saw Cody carrying fast-food bags through his backyard. Was I so deep into a depressed zombie state that I couldn't move toward someone screaming? I'm not proud of it.

Maria came running home at that point, heard the screaming, then picked up speed while running through our backyard into the alley, then ran through Karl's backyard to his sliding glass door, opened it and yelled, "Cody's hurt!" Then ran through the gate in our mutual fence and into our house to grab her keys, wallet, and phone and saw me standing in my bathrobe, holding a cup of coffee. A bad look, based on her expression. She wasted no time saying so. She ran back out and drove Cody to the emergency room and called Karl who met her there. When she got back home, I was still in my bathrobe, working on my third cup of coffee and a bowl of cereal, reading articles on my phone about optimizing stereo performance.

"What the fuck is wrong with you?" she said. "You heard him screaming, right?"

"I was sleepy," I said. "I slept in—it's Saturday."

"It's *Sunday*," she said. "He has a concussion, a broken arm, and a broken tooth. His mouth was covered in blood, some of which he left in our car that maybe you could address?"

"I'll address the blood," I said. I figured on watching a YouTube tutorial on blood-removal techniques. I did feel guilty. I felt worse for disappointing Maria than I felt for leaving Cody in the alley. That afternoon, I made a dramatic move to show Maria my newfound compassion. I asked Elvis if he needed anything from the grocery store.

"Carton of Marlboro Reds and a pint of Jack Beam," he said.

"Jim Beam? Jack Daniels?"

"George Dickel. And a boombox. Motherfuckers stole my boombox."

"Motherfuckers," I said.

I handed him a bag when I returned. No boombox.

"I'll have to pay you on the first," he said. "That okay?"

I said it was, then stepped into our kitchen to brag to Maria of my generosity. She wasn't there, but three large suitcases were. Meant for me? I found her upstairs in her craft/music room, unpacking boxes while classical music played, lots of violins.

I told her what I'd done for Elvis.

"Wonderful," she said. "You've adopted an old man you can kill off with cigarettes and booze. Doesn't he have kids— or friends, or anyone? He never has visitors."

"*We* never have visitors," I said, meaning we were okay.

"I know," Maria said, meaning we were *not* okay.

"Those suitcases in the kitchen?" I said. "Where should I put them?"

"You should fill them with your shit and take them home. *Florida*-home."

I sat on the floor of her room, gut-punched. Her job wasn't going well. Her music department consisted of insecure old men with inflated egos competing for miniscule portions of respect they'd never get from each other or from the hundreds of students required to appreciate the music they were required to inflict upon them.

"What I need is to look forward to coming home," she said. "You're not—"

"I can help with that," I said. I didn't want to beg or grovel. There were times to stand up for oneself. "Give me another chance. It'll get better."

"You either need to get a job so you can pay people to fix the house or learn to fix some things yourself while I'm working every day to pay the mortgage."

"You're right," I said. And she was. I'd been spending too much time in the basement, calibrating and rearranging speakers, feeling listless, secretly (or so I thought) depressed over seeing no way to be of any use to Maria or my neighbors or the world.

"It'll get better," I said again, as we moved toward fall.

Things got worse. In early October, about 1 a.m., we heard Karl in our front yard repeating, very softly, "I love you." We got on our knees and peeked out, saw he had Cody pinned on his stomach. Cody kept saying, "Get the fuck off me," and Karl kept saying, "I love you." Then two cop cars pulled up, no flashing lights, no sirens. They put Cody in the backseat. Karl said *I love you*, then closed the door and the cops took Cody away.

"Something's wrong over there," Maria said. "Maybe we should talk to them."

"None of our business," I said. "They'll be okay."

"There you go again," she said. "Going out of your way to offer help."

The next morning, I saw Karl watering his garden, holster over his sweatpants. I wanted to ask what happened, and I wanted to say I admired the gentle way he kept telling his son he loved him, even as he had him pinned, even as he pushed him into a cop car.

He said, "Sorry if that ruckus last night woke you guys."

"No," I said. "We hardly noticed."

"Cody's acting up lately. I called the cops so he'd learn about the consequences of his choices. Everything's fine now. Need any Swiss Chard? Or a pumpkin? It's getting to be jack-o'-lantern carving time, my favorite holiday."

What I should've said: *That's a very kind gesture.*

I said, "Swiss Chard is gross. And for Halloween, I turn off the lights and close the curtains and pretend no one's home."

"You play poker?" he said.

"Never have." This wasn't true, but I had no desire to play again.

He pointed to my garage. "Me and the guys played a lot of poker out there. We'll teach you. I've got today off before I go on for six days, so I'm going fly-fishing. We've got some world-class trout streams around here. Go with?"

"I should unpack some boxes," I said.

"Next time," he said, and turned back to watering his garden.

We could still sleep with open windows in October, but that also meant we could hear students marching home from bars, using our front yard for vomiting and urinating, squabbling and singing. Drivers stopped in front of our house long enough to pop their doors, puke in the street, then speed away. One Tuesday night at 2 a.m., a driver collided into our embankment, an explosive sound that sent all three cats sailing off the bed and down the hall. I went out in my bathrobe to see if anyone was dead. When I got there, the driver had already backed up and raced away, leaving a front bumper in our flowerbed. Neither Karl nor Kim were home, apparently, and Elvis was too deaf to have heard.

"Was anyone hurt?" Maria said, resorting to compassion.

"Unfortunately not," I said.

We wondered how people survived winter. Did they? We talked to no one. Chit-chat isn't possible when it's minus-thirty and your lips won't work and you're swatting invisible wasps because your face is burning and you become a God-cursing lunatic scowling at the gray skies that grow layers and lower themselves into your anesthetized and freezer-burned soul while the snow comes and keeps coming and the only absence of white in the deep-white world is the small gap between the snow in front yards and the snow on roofs, like a heavy-lidded eye peering out from purgatory.

But there was Karl, plow attached to truck, clearing our alley, and there he was with his snowblower clearing his side-walk and ours. I waved my appreciation and kept moving. Stupidly, we studied the calendar, sang Merle Haggard's "If We Make it Through December," changed the lyric to January, then February, then over Maria's spring break we took our bikes to a trail still unpassable from ice and returned home, defeated. Snow melted in the day and refroze overnight, and we slipped and fell on sidewalks, people broke wrists and hips. The trees held the same grudge we did and refused to wake. Then in April, the sun appeared, then snow, sun, snow, then sun without warmth, then on May 15th, we stepped outside and took our first deep breath in seven months and said, "Is this—could it be—March?"

So we survived, and spring exploded into summer with its soft mornings and long days, and we finished unpacking (slowed by my laziness), opened windows, built raised bed gardens, planted and watered vegetables, hired a contractor to build a retaining wall to keep drunk drivers out of our living room, planted bigger shrubs to shield us from the street, bought a twenty-foot elm from a tree nursery who planted it between our side-kitchen window and Elvis's side stoop so we couldn't see each other. Gladys barked at the workers. Elvis said, "She ain't nothing but a hound dog." And we laughed, and thought, for a moment, things might be okay.

Things got worse.

The last Saturday of June, after working in the flowerbeds, after showers and a simple dinner, we sat in the living room in front of a movie we'd been waiting for. It was dusk, both of us on the couch, windows closed, curtains drawn, three cats between us, and Maria was knitting for the first time since we'd moved, resuming work on a sweater, and I pressed "play."

"Mute it," she said. "I heard something."

I should've muted it. I should've said, "Let's take a look." I said, "It's just the TV."

She reached behind her to open the curtains.

"It's not the TV," she said.

I sighed, pressed pause. Looked. In our flowerbed, leaning against our house, stood a uniformed cop with his gun drawn, pointed skyward, facing Karl's house. When he saw me looking at him—we were eye to eye, one foot apart—he put an index finger to his lips. He looked past me toward the television, concentrating, something sad in his eyes like he wanted nothing more than to join us on our couch. He looked back toward Karl's, and I turned to Maria, but she was gone. She was upstairs packing, preparing our evacuation.

Another cop stood on the far side of Karl's house, crouched behind a tree, gun pulled and pointed up. In the street, two cop cars were parked nose-to-nose, blocking traffic on the north end of the block. Two other cars blocked traffic on the south end of the block. I went to the kitchen, looked across our backyards. Two cops were standing in our rear flowerbed, guns pulled. In the alley—on Karl's side—a BearCat had pulled up and a team of guys in black jumpsuits squatted behind it, holding rifles.

Maria came back carrying a duffel bag, said, "Let's run out the back."

I should've said, *Good idea.*

"No way," I said. "Cops are always overreacting." I figured it was some minor misunderstanding Karl would soon rectify, the entire squadron would soon disperse, we could resume our movie, and I'd get the whole silly scoop tomorrow while Karl watered his garden.

I looked out the back window. The alley light between our garages flickered on. Then one cop said something to another, and they lowered their heads while the first cop raised his rifle and shot out the light. His gun didn't make a sound, but the glass shattered and rained down, bounced off the armored BearCat and the concrete alley. I was glad Maria hadn't seen it.

"Holy fuck," Maria said. She was behind me, bag in hand. She said, "Let's go."

I studied the layout, the logistics of moving through potential crossfire.

A loud knock erupted on the front door. I looked at Maria and walked that way.

"Ask who it is," she said.

"Who is it?" I said.

"Captain Morgan," the voice said.

Like the rum, I wondered? If we'd had a peephole, I would've peeped. Maria had noticed this on our walkthrough with our real estate agent who assured us there was no need for a peephole in such a safe neighborhood in a city where crime was low, etc.

I opened the door. A uniformed cop looked over my shoulder into the house.

"How many in your home?" he said.

"Two humans and three cats," I said.

"All accounted for?"

"Roger," I said, then felt dumb for using such language. Also, the cats were indoor cats, but I didn't bother explaining.

"You need to run out the back, continue north and stay clear until we notify you that the environment is secure."

"What's going on?" I said. Why was the environment insecure?

"We have a situation," said Captain Obvious.

"Let's go," Maria said.

"Is it Cody?" I said. "The oldest kid?"

"I'm not at liberty to disclose. Mr. Hanson is alone with a firearm he could potentially discharge in this direction. He's communicating via cellphone with a crisis mediator who reports that he's alternating between suicidal ideation and intense hostility that developed when he learned his wife is having an affair with a younger coworker, but that's all I can tell you."

"Maybe I should talk to him," I said.

"Let's go," Maria said. "He doesn't want to talk to you."

"She's right," Captain Morgan said. "He doesn't want to talk to you."

"Get your keys and lock the door," Maria said. "I'm leaving food for the cats."

"He might talk to me," I said.

"You 're not friends," Maria said. "He tried to be friends, but you brushed him off."

Was I hearing that this forced evacuation was *my* fault? I knew I shouldn't ask.

"So you're blaming *me*?" I said. I looked at Captain Morgan to see if he'd corroborate the silliness of this accusation.

"Not a good time for a domestic dispute," Captain Morgan said.

"Get your wallet and phone," Maria said. "Tie your shoes. How old are you?"

"Good luck to you both," Captain Morgan said, and walked out the front.

We walked out the back and down the alley and headed north. We neared the corner tavern, front door propped open, so I pointed. It looked like a cozy place to hide out for a couple of hours until things blew over.

"We're going to a motel," Maria said, and increased her pace, like she knew exactly where she was going. Like she'd been there before.

"Have you gone here before?" I said.

"Sure," she said. "With Elvis. Then Karl. Then both Karl and Elvis."

It was a two-level job, charcoal grills outside some doors on the ground level. She requested a room on the second floor, and gave them a credit card, $69 per night, with cable, two beds. I flopped onto one, Maria on the other. She picked a couple of things off the bedspread.

"Disgusting," she said. "People have smoked in here. Do *not* get beneath the covers. Don't touch the remote control."

I grabbed the remote control and started flipping. "Poor Karl," I said.

"Poor *Karl?* Karl is a fucking asshole who has forced us into this disease-ridden dump."

I should've said, "You're right. That's not good."

I said, "He may have walked in on them and lost it."

"No excuse for violence. Or to threaten violence. If you don't see that, we're done."

She got on her phone, started looking for what? Flights? Ubers? New partners?

A bickering couple came through the wall, a man and woman going at it, voices escalating as she called him a dirty motherfucker and he called her a stupid cunt, then a sound like a body slammed against a wall, then a door slam, then quiet.

"Charming," Maria said.

"This motel reminds me of a motel my father and I stayed in one summer when I was visiting him and his fifth wife, when she kicked him out and we stayed there for a week."

"Please," she said. "Not memory lane right now."

"I'm getting a little tired of your negativity," I said. "I'm trying—"

"Stop talking. If one more thing goes wrong, I might have to hurt you."

I watched the nature channel, slo-mo lions chasing down slo-mo gazelles to a horror movie soundtrack. Then dozed off. At midnight, my phone rang.

"Captain Morgan here," said the voice. He sounded tired and bored. Great police work though, I thought, to have found my phone number. He said, "Is there a vantage point in your house—a window that provides visual access into your neighbor's home?"

Would I be confessing to voyeurism if I said yes? The window was upstairs in Maria's craft and music room, where she'd set up her harp, her loom, her sewing machine, bins of yarn arranged by strand and color. This room had been her first priority, her sacred space. But yes, I had seen through that window into a room in Karl's house crammed with scattered debris, and I had seen a light go on and his legs enter and move around, then leave again, lights back off.

"What's going on?" Maria said.

"Yes," I told Captain Morgan. "Upstairs. First door on the left."

"You didn't lock the door, did you?" Maria said.

I thought I had. Maybe I hadn't.

Captain Morgan said, "The door is currently unlocked, we noticed. Do we have permission to enter your home to conduct a brief surveillance mission?"

"Tell him *no*," Maria said.

"We have three cats," I said. I tried to sound stern, a tough negotiator, but my voice had always been on the soft side. "The black cat is especially sneaky when the door opens."

He hung up. Maria punched me in the shoulder. Hard. "You just let the whole fucking SWAT team into our house and into *my* room? With the cats there?"

"They'll hide," I said. "It's a brief surveillance mission."

"Oh, Christ," she said.

I forgot what SWAT stood for. I looked it up. Special Weapons And Tactics team. They would have to move her harp. And her loom, which was already holding a project she'd started the day after we moved in because that's what kept her sane, she said. Now men with guns were tromping their boots upstairs across our carpet and into her room where delicate things were arranged delicately. I knew better than to say anything.

I said, "It'll be over soon, and we'll be back home."

"Home?" She laughed a little laugh I knew would break open her tear ducts, and she went into the bathroom and locked the door.

I didn't say anything else. My phone woke me at 4 a.m. Captain Morgan said the area was secure and we could return home.

My first question should've been, *Is everyone okay?*

I said, "What happened?"

"I'm not at liberty to disclose, but once Mr. Hanson threatened self-harm, an officer entered the residence, at which time Mr. Hanson discharged his firearm into multiple walls, including the south-facing wall that faces your home, and then our crisis mediator established contact and applied his training to pacify Mr. Hanson into surrender, but that's all I can tell you."

I thanked him and hung up. To Maria, I said, "The area is secure. Let's go."

"Too dark," she said. "We'll wait."

We waited. In a couple of hours, she woke me. Soft light came through the window. We left and started walking. Except for the shattered streetlight still scattered in the alley, there was no sign of what had happened the night before. Once inside, Maria counted cats. They were hiding, but they responded to her voice, not mine, and in a little while they came out. Maria checked the condition of her craft room. I took a cap off the rack and put it on, and when I did, all three cats sprinted away.

After stumbling through the day sleep-deprived, grumpy and stupid, we got into our own beds, turned on our lamps and each started reading. A bat joined us. Maria pulled the covers up while I got the net, crouched, and tried to snag it without killing it. I killed it.

She said, "If one more fucking thing goes wrong, I'm going to lose it."

"Nothing else could go wrong," I said.

At 2 a.m., we woke to gunshots—or what we thought were gunshots—outside our open window. The cats scampered and Maria fell out of bed and crawled around to my side, telling me to get down between the bed and wall. I crawled to the window to look out.

She said, "Keep your head down."

I looked out. Cody was in the street with two other guys throwing things on the asphalt that exploded. "Fireworks," I said. "They're throwing down those firecracker things that pop when they hit the ground."

"Trying to scare us," she said. "Definitely on purpose. If I were you, I'd call the cops."

"If you were me."

"They'll call me hysterical, think I'm overreacting. They'll take *you* seriously because you have a dick, dick."

I didn't call the cops. We went another night without sleep. The next afternoon, bass drums came from Karl's backyard so loud it rattled our windows. Cody and three of his friends stood in a circle, smoking, caps crooked, jeans below their underwear, holding cans of beer, a twelve pack at their feet, laughing loudly, and still, over the music, we heard them say things like *fucking motherfucker say fuck that motherfucking fucker of a fuckhead motherfucker.*

Maria said, "If I were you, I'd go talk to Cody. See if he's okay. Tell him you're here if he needs an adult in his life."

I didn't want to. I'd antagonize them. There was no winning once they felt contempt for the authority figure they believed was patronizing them. I knew the feeling. They'd sabotage our peace and retaliate like guerrilla warriors with flaming poop on the doorstep, sand in the gas tank, hit-and-run doorbell attacks at 3 a.m., a slashed tire or two.

Maria looked at me, said, "Well?"

I didn't move. I opened my mouth, then closed it.

She stormed out the kitchen door, marched across the backyard and stopped at the fence, hands on hips. She said, "Hey!" just once. They turned down the music and faced her.

I watched from the open window, ready to help if she needed help.

She said, "Cody, come here, please."

Cody didn't want to take orders, but he shuffled to the fence, turned sideways, looked toward his feet. He was just sixteen, delicate and scared, ready to receive a hug or throw a punch, incapable of knowing the word for either. It would be a chore to get a single word from him.

Maria said, "Are you okay?"

"Yeah," he said, dragging out the syllable. "I'm straight."

"Where are your parents?"

And here, a glimpse of resentment for the interrogation.

"Mom says she's working, but I don't know. Dad—they took him away for a minute."

"He'll be okay. Sounds like he was going through a rough time, but he'll be okay."

"Yeah, he went crazy in the head a little bit."

"He'll be okay," Maria repeated. "In the meantime, let's make a deal."

I was impressed with her candor, the way she was reaching out to him, offering help. A crisis negotiator. He looked at her then, full eye contact, almost ready for a hug.

She said, "If you keep things quiet over here—no fireworks in the street late at night, no loud music outside—then we'll have no reason to call the cops." She got close then, cocked her head, and said, very seriously and with wide eyes: "You feel me?"

He looked down, not sure what to do with this.

Then she said, "But also, listen—if you need anything—food, whatever, let us know."

He paused again. Said, "Sorry about the fireworks. I ain't mean to scare nobody." He looked sincere. He hadn't thought about it. She was on the verge of adopting him.

"Okay," Maria said. "Let us know if we can help."

"Bet," he said.

When she turned and walked toward the house, Cody's friend handed him a beer and performed a pelvis thrust in her direction. I didn't tell her.

"See," she said. "That's how you act like an adult who wants to help someone."

"Nice job," I said. "Can we have tacos?"

That night, another bat. I tried to shoo it outside with a box lid and killed it. So delicate, so small, all shriveled up like that, a little brown bat big as a mouse. Also, sounds from the closet. Hangers sliding, old lady Lang arranging her wardrobe. We didn't mention it anymore.

The next morning, we were up at 6 a.m. again while Elvis hacked and Gladys barked. We poured our first cup of coffee and looked out back, saw Cody lean out the second-floor window of Karl's garage, shirtless, holding a rifle. He puked over our fence into our flowerbed. A group of about six guys came out of the garage then, went to a car that had just pulled down the alley, passed something through the window in exchange for something else.

Maria started packing. At 8 a.m., she contacted a different real estate agent, got our house listed, marked it down so it would sell quickly, and we prepared ourselves for a loss.

And it did sell quickly—within two weeks, at a loss, during which time we didn't see Karl. We bought a house across town we couldn't afford. One that would force me to get a job. But there were trees. A porch. Space. Quiet. Deer in the backyard, orioles, a pileated woodpecker. We unpacked. We survived another winter, bought new coats, firewood, snowshoes, a new furnace.

A year later, we threw a house-warming party also meant to ingratiate Maria to the department members who would vote on her tenure, her job security, our ability to buy more appliances. We spent three hundred dollars on beer, wine, bourbon, scotch, and cheese, and people came. And stayed. I played the good host, made my rounds clutching my non-alcoholic beer, and at 10 p.m. found myself in the basement behind the built-in bar the previous owners had installed, empty-handed and cornered by Maria's department chair, a sixty-year-old man who started crying while he talked of the mistake he'd made thirty years ago moving from New York City, how his wife had realized the mistake early on and left him here. He talked about the futility of his profession, of life generally, and he confided that just last week he had tried to kill himself, preferring the garden hose from the tailpipe into the car method, but when he went to find the hose, he discovered he didn't own one—that he had *never* owned one. Then he touched my shoulder and asked if I'd be a good friend and loan him mine. It was the quality of his laughter that made me reach for the whiskey. I poured him some, then me.

Maria found me on the bathroom floor. People were gone, the house a wreck. I vomited until nothing came out, then kept vomiting. She kept asking if I was okay, but I couldn't answer. This wasn't your standard drunk-vomiting—I'd done that a few dozen times since high school and knew the feeling well—this was some weird new dangerous vomiting that was killing me, a half-bottle of scotch consumed rapidly, chased by an allergic reaction that had me close to convulsions. Maria said, "Oh boy." She sounded a little tipsy herself, but at least she was upright. I hoped she'd had a good time.

"Dith you've a time?" I said.

"Damnit," she said.

On the bathroom tile, I tried with my finger to outline "911" thinking she'd figure it out. She didn't. I used my finger to say come closer, and when she came closer, I explained.

"I can't understand you," she said. "I'm calling 911."

She put a cold rag on my head. Two men came in the house. My eyes were closed, but I thought I could tell from the voices that one of them was Karl. Later, Maria told me it wasn't Karl, that I had imagined it. At the time, in my drunk-dream, I felt Karl grab my wrist and tell me I'd be okay while I apologized for causing trouble and he said, "Believe it or not, I've seen worse." Then I had my arm around his shoulder and he had an arm around my side, almost like a hug, while he carried me out, and I tried to tell him how sorry I was about not helping Cody that time, and how much I admired him, that I was even jealous of how easy it was for him to help people, and he said, "Hush up now."

In the months after, I thought of Karl every time I heard a siren. When firetrucks blared by, I looked to see who was driving, whether Karl was inside the cab. I never saw him. I'd taken a third-shift job at a hospital in Environmental Services (a custodian) and got my nightly dose of death, those on the brink and those fighting against it, including all the exhausted nurses. The nurses never made eye contact while I pushed my cart down the halls and into and out of rooms, and that was okay. I told no one that I'd once been one of them, that I knew how those twelve-hour shifts drained your spirit and made you ache for outside air and sleep. I came to enjoy (if enjoy is the word) those long and quiet nights where my job meant keeping clean the places where people performed the more important jobs of tending to folks they wanted to release.

One snowy morning near Christmas, I completed a thorough cleaning of a room where a young woman had died, where her family had circled her bedside and sobbed, and when my shift ended, I found myself wanting to do some small good thing for someone which might also make *me* feel better. In the parking lot, with snow falling and the forecast calling for another foot, I drove to a hardware store and bought a snowblower (though Maria's advice had been to buy one at the end of the previous winter, when they'd be cheaper). Inside the store, I passed through the hunting and fishing section and saw a long-handled net, which made me think of Karl and the net he'd loaned me that I'd cut a hole in. I decided to buy him a new one. Yes, a strange mood.

I drove to his house to deliver it. If he wasn't home, I'd leave it on his porch, let him guess who it was from. If he couldn't guess, all the better, I thought, in the spirit of the so-called Good Samaritan committing anonymous acts of goodness. He wouldn't think it a big deal, most likely. Just how we do things here, I'd tell him. I'd avoided driving by our old house since we'd moved. I didn't want to revisit the ghosts. From a block away, I saw three For Sale signs lined up—one in Karl's yard, one in our old yard, and one in Elvis's yard. Strips of siding had peeled away from Karl's house and plywood covered each of the downstairs windows. The front doorknob had a padlock around it. No cars were in the alley. The house looked like it had been vacant a long time. Our old house, for sale by a different company, had aged too, hedges gone wild, a missing shutter, peeling paint. Had Elvis died? Finally? Alongside Gladys? It was strange, three consecutive houses for sale, the kind of thing you see in a town where the water goes bad, or a big company shuts down.

I drove to the fire station where Karl worked, feeling more curious than noble. The snow was heavier, but I'd gotten use to driving in it. I watched a big firetruck back into the garage, returning from a call, and the men started filing out of it. Karl was not among them. I must've looked strange, carrying a long fishing net through the falling snow.

"Looking for butterflies?" one guy said.

"No, I'm—is Karl working today?"

"Karl? Karl *Hanson*?"

How many Karls could there be working in one fire station?

"Karl's no longer with us," the guy said.

"He's at a different station?"

He stared at me, eyes narrowing. I imagined he was one of the guys who had played poker with Karl in my old garage before it was my garage, someone who had worked alongside Karl on tough calls late at night, maybe saved a life or two together.

"He's—were you a friend of his?"

I guess I couldn't say that, not really. "We used to be neighbors. I owe him a net."

"He's no longer with us." He didn't want to reveal anything else.

I nodded, carried the net back to my car and put it on top of my snowblower and drove home through the snow, falling heavier now, piling up quickly. It was strange, but I looked for Karl everywhere, thinking he might appear on a random street corner. But he was no longer with us. Meaning dead? Later, I searched online, adding "obituary" to his name, as I did occasionally with folks I'd lost touch with, and nothing came up.

On the corner adjacent to my house, I spotted the old lady I'd seen before, slipping in her driveway, falling to one knee. I parked and went to her, helped her into her house, which wasn't hard. She was old and thin, not heavy. She said something about dialysis, something about her grandchildren at school, something about having no help since her husband died and left her alone, something about carrots in the pot roast.

I put her on the couch and went to her kitchen, found a piece of paper where I wrote my name and number, then went back to her on the couch. "I'll be your first responder," I said.

I moved a blanket from the back of a chair over her, and went out to shovel her driveway with the shovel propped against her house, me with no gloves and a nose and toes raised in Florida. Who wouldn't do the same? Then I shoveled the driveway next to mine that belonged to Joe, a doctor who'd had his foot run over by a man in a truck, then I tended to the driveway on the other side, owned by a Vietnam Vet who voted for idiots, my new snowblower still in the box, still without gloves, without a hat, in tennis shoes, so cold I couldn't feel my hands, but I kept at it, doing what needed to be done before I went home to check on my own crock pot I'd prepared that morning, packed with vegetables and broth and seasonings like liquid smoke, thyme, and paprika that I hoped Maria would say smelled wonderful when she walked in. But just then, while I shoveled, I thought of people with worse luck, the dead and the dying, the incarcerated and the disabled, all of them jealous of where I was, doing what I was doing.

Hurricane Zelda,
a Dad Like Driftwood,
a Vulture Named Claude

Maria knew her mother would not evacuate, but she called once more (the third time in two hours) from 1,400 miles away and begged her, yet again, to leave her thin-walled and tree-surrounded home in Florida before Zelda—category 5 and strengthening, ETA four hours—came to kill her. And yet again, her mother said, "Mind your own business. If Zelda kills me, I can say it meant God wanted me to die where I was born."

"There are less violent ways," Maria said. "I can help with that."

"I'm sure you could," May said. "I'm just going to pray and button down the hatches."

"*Batten* down the hatches," Maria said.

"Maybe you could pray a little too, for once," May said.

Maria half-listened to her mother repeat how tired she was of leaving and returning from so many hurricanes, tired of the filthy motel rooms like the one she'd fled to three months ago near Tallahassee, where the prices had doubled and the bed bugs pushed her to the floor, and she woke with flea bites on her neck, which meant her mutt, Toto, had brought them home to multiply. With any luck, May said, the fleas would soon be gone with the wind. She repeated that she lived 1.2 miles west of I-95, which meant she wasn't violating the mandatory evacuation orders the Governor issued for those *east* of I-95.

"I've left the house and everything in it to you," she said.

"How generous," said Maria, an only child. "To inherit a blown-away house."

"I bet you don't even want it based on how you act about coming home, like you've gotten above your raisin'. You should have some humbleness."

"You mean humility. I should have *humility*."

"Yes, you should."

Maria's partner, Marty, was hearing this over speakerphone from their living room in Wisconsin, shaking his head at May's stubbornness. He'd been shaking his head before that too, as he did every morning, one eye on his newsfeed, one eye on TV news, binge-drinking coffee in his underwear while fueling his rage at the rich fucks who failed to acknowledge environmental racism or climate-change refugees, his areas of interest these days as a self-labeled freelance (non-working) journalist and full-time talker too paralyzed with despair to cook or clean or change a light bulb. They'd been together six years, had been in Wisconsin three years, and for the past year, he'd been on the couch, in his underwear, on his phone, tracking their extinction.

"It's just a house," Maria said. "Not even a good one." It was a clapboard shack with sheetrock walls May's parents built in a hurry in 1933, nestled beneath brittle trees that would splinter like toothpicks, branches heavy as bombs. Maria lived in the house for eighteen years before college, and what she concluded then, thirty years ago, was that it was worth leaving.

"Your father's here," May said.

"Don't call him that. I've never met the man."

Two months ago, May's first and only husband, Maria's father, appeared on her porch "like washed-up driftwood," she said, then handed her a bouquet of flowers from Winn-Dixie and asked about the trailer behind May's house. It had belonged to her older brother, Mark, who'd died the previous summer, and she'd left it unchanged, still furnished. Sure, she told him, he could stay awhile if he traded out rent for handyman jobs. Maria knew the story. How he kept asking for forgiveness for leaving his pregnant wife with her parents fifty years ago, for vanishing, for never once calling. Maria kept waiting for him to murder May, steal whatever was worth stealing and vanish.

"He offered to take me away," May said. "I said I was staying, so he said he'd stay with me. He said we could go out together in a blaze of glory like Butch Cassidy and what's-his-name. He's kind of romantic, actually, not that I—"

"You should have flown up here," Maria said.

Marty laughed from the living room. May laughed from Florida. She laughed and couldn't stop laughing. "Oh, but wouldn't that be fun?" she said.

May had never been on a plane, and she wasn't about to die in a crash when she could die in a hurricane instead. Even if she entertained the idea long enough to be revived after hearing the cost, she'd say what about Toto and how would Maria feel if *she* was in a crate that long? Two years ago, when May and Mark returned from evacuating Wilma, they found the mutt on her front porch, no collar, and named her Toto, splitting no hairs between Kansas-based tornados and Atlantic-brewed hurricanes.

"If I don't make it and Toto does, you have to adopt her," May said.

"Toto's on her own," Maria said. She wasn't about to pick up frozen poop through a Wisconsin winter. May had given up asking why she didn't evacuate those winters, and weren't there lots of schools closer where she could teach her singing lessons? "*Classes*," Maria kept correcting. "I teach classes in vocal performance in the Theatre department of a state university." Then she'd explain, once more, how she'd finally stumbled into a tenure-track job after a decade of part-time adjunct work without benefits and how she'd come to appreciate the first snows of winter and the reflective mood her mind moved toward and how such winters made spring explode with spirit-filled wonder. Then May would call her "uppity-sounding," and Maria would say, "Gotta go," and hang up.

Now, Maria said, "How am I supposed to help you?"

"*Pray*, honey."

"Gotta go," Maria said, and hung up. She and Marty watched the looped footage of Zelda leveling the Bahamas, where *dozens* were reported dead, *scores* missing.

"Remember when President Dickhead tossed out paper towels in Puerto Rico?" Marty said. "I wish Zelda would demolish *his* place."

"I don't feel well," Maria said. A wave of pressure emerged in her head, a recurring wave she'd seen doctors about a few days ago, where initial tests determined that further testing was necessary, none of which she'd told her mother about. She suspected a softball-sized tumor had taken root in fertile brain tissue, stretching her skull, but she didn't want to worry her mother.

"The rich and powerful throw paper towels at poor people after hurricanes," Marty said.

"I have to lie down," Maria said, but didn't move.

Marty wanted to evacuate to Denmark while hoping for a Wall Street collapse that would force super-rich Republicans to stand in soup lines and get a taste of poverty. Unless they jumped from buildings first because the soup wasn't fresh, which would be a start on what really needed to happen, that the octogenarians in charge die off. Maria didn't disagree entirely, she just wished he'd be quiet long enough to take her to a concert or an art museum or on a bike ride beside the beautiful Mississippi River or to a decent dinner somewhere that required pants.

An hour later, they remained on the couch watching footage that switched between *the devastation* of the Bahamas and a rain-battered weather dramatist in northern Florida dressed in a yellow coat holding on to his yellow hat, squatted beside a flapping stop sign, warning viewers that wicked winds were worsening.

The phone Maria held in her hands vibrated with her mother's call.

"I'd like Tanya Tucker played at my funeral," May said.

"I can't allow that," Maria said. "When it gets bad, lie in the tub."

"We're already there, honey. Toto's shaking. Have you been praying?"

Maria was—with the exception of a few Gregorian chants that spoke to some ancient mystery she didn't care to analyze—devoutly agnostic. "Fill your washing machine and your sinks with water," she said.

"I'm also filling the tub with water."

"Keep your phone charged so you can call 911."

"I'll meet you at his mansion in the sky," May said.

"I'll talk to you later."

"We'll see about that."

Marty changed the channel to C-Span, which made Maria want to leave and take a walk to the river with Jessye Norman in her ears, but it was raining again, or still. Wasn't it? The curtains were closed. Windows too. She was aware suddenly that the ceiling seemed to have sunk. The walls were too close. Marty was also too close. Had he showered this week? A new wave of pressure rose in her head, then her phone dinged with texts from May, complete with hashtags because she'd learned this was the cool thing to do.

Walls r shaking. #neednewunderwear

I hear that train a-coming. #movingtowardthelight #howhighsthewatermama?

Big pecan tree bit the dust. #nutbuster

My Buick got squashed. #takemenowlord.

Forgive me my sins. #areyoupraying?

Play some Dolly too. #iwillalwaysloveyou

Maria yanked the remote from Marty and turned back to the Weather Channel.

"You realize," she said, "my mother is in the middle of a fucking hurricane?"

"Congress is emasculating the EPA," Marty said. "We're officially past the fucked point. The refugees Zelda will create are also fucked, at least for the few years it'll take FEMA to do the paperwork. Where will your mother go?"

Where *would* her mother go if her house was gone? If it meant staying in Florida, she'd prefer a flooded nursing home over a Wisconsin winter.

Zelda crashed into Jacksonville: walls of sideways-moving rain joined ocean waves that smacked the boarded-up and empty Landing-area. Palm trees lost their heads. Waves leapt silly sandbags and sent dumpsters sailing down streets like pinballs. May lived twenty miles north of what Maria was seeing, but it couldn't be better there. She texted her. Nothing. Maybe she'd lost service, maybe she was dead. Her phone kept going to voicemail. She scrolled social media for local news. Nothing. Because no one was there. She messaged a boyfriend from twenty years ago, Leonard, asked if he could check on her mother. No reply. Did he still believe she had a superiority complex? The footage cut to the damage visible south of Jacksonville: a trailer park converted to a landfill, boat on a roof, mattress in a tree, a crater beneath an uprooted oak that squashed two roofs and made the houses themselves invisible.

"We're going to need more paper towels," Marty said.

Two hours later, her phone rang. She muted the TV and answered.

"Hey, baby," said a southern-sounding man with a slimy-sounding whisper.

"Who's this?"

"It's your Daddy, honey."

"Where's Mom?"

"We've had some damage."

"Put her on," Maria said.

"The big pecan tree blew down and killed her Buick."

"Put her on."

"She sat in the tub squeezing Toto and I crouched in behind her squeezing Katrina—that's my deaf old Yorkie. And we all held on to each other and prayed 'till it passed. I think she's got the shell-shock, honey. I'm sitting on the toilet here next to her now, and she's in the tub asking me to take her home. I wonder if you might ought to come check on her, help us clean up a little bit if you're able."

Maria was already online, looking at flights, calculating Zelda's speed as it tracked toward Savannah and Charleston. She said, "I'm coming. Tell her I'm coming."

"I'm going to give her something to help her sleep, but listen."

"Pick me up at the airport tomorrow, 5 p.m."

"Yeah, but listen."

"What?"

"Could you bring me a wheel of smoked Gouda?"

Maria hung up, booked the flight, stretching her credit card.

Marty said, "That was your *father*? Let me take a wild guess on *his* party affiliation."

"I don't feel well," she said. "I assumed you didn't want to go with me?"

"We can't afford it," Marty said. "And also, no."

She went to bed, set her alarm for the early flight that would take all day with two stops, slept little. Marty, who had slept well, drove her to the airport, listening to NPR's assessment of the damage so loudly Maria had to turn it off, preferring silence, a chance for Marty to ask how she was feeling. He didn't. She kept her eyes closed, pressure building in her head again. Her next medical tests were a week away; she'd be back in plenty of time.

She didn't sleep on the small plane to Minneapolis, nor on the big plane to Atlanta, nor during her three-hour layover, nor the one-hour flight to Jacksonville. She wore a mask, but the coughers and sneezers didn't, and by the time she arrived, she felt like her head had ingested a cloud that kept swelling, inflated by the requisite travel Valium and Bloody Mary. She'd stepped out of Wisconsin at 63 degrees with long pants and long sleeves, then stepped into Florida's 102 degrees, humidity that clutched her throat and dunked her in a heated swamp. She instantly broke a sweat and felt embarrassed for doing so, as if her hometown air was mocking her, saying, "You been away too long and done got soft, little girl." Two topless palm trees stood nearby like burnt torches. Other passengers in shorts, t-shirts, and sandals were picked up by people who greeted them with hugs and laughs, golf clubs loaded into trunks.

A fully electric car (she knew by its quietness) pulled up in front of her, and a skinny old man in a pink shirt and a long white beard emerged from it and walked toward her, smiling, showing perfect white teeth. A wiry-looking guy with good posture, lifting his arms now like he meant to hug her. She backed away.

"It's me, honey," he said. "Your dear 'ol Daddy. You look just like your mama."

"No I don't."

She rolled her suitcase to the rear of the car, and he beat her there, lifted the trunk door and hoisted her bag in for her, gasping from the effort.

"I'm going to take you home, sweetheart," he said.

She didn't feel like talking and had no plans to do so. She opened the passenger side door and saw the seat occupied by a small dog who wagged its tail, and when Maria picked her up and sat, the dog stood on her lap, turned a circle, then lay down. From the car and the dog, she smelled shampoo, pine trees, wintergreen, salt air. The man who claimed to be her father got in and stroked the dog's neck.

"Trina just had her eighteenth birthday," he said. "I found her during Hurricane Katrina when she was a puppy, and we've been together ever since. She's deaf as I am, but that means we agree on everything." He laughed at himself. A high-pitched and too-sharp laugh, accented with madness, or so it seemed to Maria, whose head was a cloud.

"Ain't life strange?" he said. "How things turn out? I'm glad I had sense enough to come back home and spend my last little bit of time on Earth with your mother. I've asked her to forgive me for leaving y'all so long ago, and she says she has. I hope you'll forgive me too. How do you like my electric vehicle?"

She didn't like that it wasn't moving. May's house was twenty miles away.

"It's *pre*-owned," he said, as if to suggest he wouldn't covet an extravagant model. "Something else I got from my dead ex-wife, but I believe everybody ought to have one. The oil companies have ruined everything." He moved gingerly ahead, checking mirrors, careful not to run over an insect. Her cloudy head confused the motion with moving through the sky. She flipped her visor down, cursed herself for forgetting sunglasses. One half of the nearest billboard was gone, the other half showed the ocean.

"My trailer got blown over," he said. "But we're lucky. We sat in the tub and held on to each other and prayed our asses off. Your mother's taught me how to pray a little. Sometimes in the evening we'd sit under that pecan tree and pray and watch the birds. That tree's gone, her car's gone, my trailer's gone, and her roof's gone, but we're lucky."

"Her roof's gone?" Maria said. Was this the first time she'd heard this?

"Very lucky," he said.

Power poles leaned over ditches like discarded crosses. Lines hung loose, one lay disconnected. Trees were splintered and uprooted, limbs scattered in piles already raked from the road. At an intersection, red lights sagged and blinked and traffic moved slowly over blown debris. The strange man beside her couldn't stop talking.

"We were squeezed up in that tub, holding on to each other and our dogs—didn't have power, of course, and it was dark, honey. I mean, *dark*. Next thing you know we felt this kind of suction like the tops of our heads was getting pulled up to the sky, which was the roof being blown off. We figured on dying right there in the tub, in each other's arms."

Soon to be a country hit, Maria thought: "Dying in the Tub, in Each Other's Arms."

"When we didn't die, we thanked the Lord and I helped your mother to bed, and we just lay right there awhile looking at the stars. You hungry? You look like you're about to dry up."

It took her awhile to hear the question. "No," she said.

"Waffle House opened back up if you want something. It's a little greasy for my taste, but we'll stop and get something if you're hungry."

"No," she said. They were on Highway 17 now, moving between snapped pines and small houses, yards sprayed with scrap lumber and trash, a tin-roof peeled back, a mattress in a ditch, enough Spanish moss blown down to make the ground look gray.

"You bring me a wheel of Gouda? I love that stuff. I traveled through there years ago after Katrina. Did some long-haul trucking, coast to coast, saw some beautiful things. Loved going through the Badlands up your way. You been there?"

She hadn't, but he couldn't hear, so she didn't answer. She recognized the houses they passed now as those she'd passed so many times so long ago, newer junked cars parked beside older junked cars. How were these houses still standing? They weren't leaning so much as sinking, rotting, swallowed up by vines and tree-high hedges, wrapped in webs of moss. Three Christmases ago, Marty had come with her, said a hurricane might improve the place. Said he'd be okay never returning.

"Your mother had her mind set on staying and I didn't want her to be alone, so I told her I'd stay with her as long as she didn't try to seduce me, which she thought was the funniest thing she'd ever heard. I'm grateful to her being so good to me. I've done some bad things, honey."

"Don't call me *honey*." She pressed a finger to each side of her temple, closed her eyes.

"Me and your Uncle Mark, we used to steal gas together. Back in high school. We snuck into the woods and stole gas from the pulpwooders back when they left their trucks and tools there overnight. We were the ones made them think the world was turning rotten, which it was. I stole it so it'd slow them down from taking so many longleaf pines, but your Uncle Mark just wanted riding-around gas. Then he found Jesus and I went to Louisiana and did some bad things. I've asked the Lord to forgive me and he has."

This road they were on was the same road she'd taken to high school in the Chevy S-10 her Uncle Mark bought at an auction and repaired for her. She parked it at the far side of the school parking lot among guys who talked passionately of rims, tires, mufflers, who made engine sounds with their mouths, who competed for loudest stereo, who made fun of

Maria's small truck, its rusted fenders, sagging rear bumper, and spider-webbing windshield crack.

"Please stop talking," she said. "I have a bad headache."

"After Katrina, I borrowed some money for a new boat, then BP spilled that oil, and then I turned as mean as a two-headed rattlesnake and drove to Houston and tracked down an oil-executive big-wig, and I hurt him, honey. Let's just say he can't walk too well anymore. I shouldn't have done it like that, but I've asked the Lord to forgive me. I left in a hurry and drifted around for work—drove a truck to Alaska, California—you ever been on that Pacific Highway? Beautiful. Settled down for a little bit in Maine but had to leave out of there in a hurry too, then I came home, told your mother I needed her forgiveness so I could die in peace. She gave me your Uncle Mark's trailer, which is totaled, so I'm going to ask if I can move in with her. Just between you and me, I'm thinking about proposing marriage. Wouldn't that be something? We're none of us doing too well if you want to know the truth about it. Your mama will lie and tell you everything's fine, but my liver's shot and her heart's weak and just between us, I think she's getting the demetria."

He meant dementia, but there was no point in pointing that out.

"I might have a brain tumor," Maria offered.

"I've always had a soft spot for your mama, and I think she's always had one for me. I shouldn't have done y'all the way I did way back then, but the Lord forgave me, and I hope you will too. I understand you're a talented singer and you teach people how to sing. You probably got your talent from me." He laughed at himself. "I hear you got a good job and a decent man. Is he a good listener? A good listener's hard to find. Your mama tells me that all the time."

They passed the dark-mouthed entrance to Seashore Trailer Park, crumbling asphalt disappearing into a cave where her former boyfriend (who still hadn't replied to her message) had lived. She went there after her Winn-Dixie night shifts—she was a high school senior and he was the thirty-year-old manager—to smoke pot and listen to albums on his good stereo—Jefferson Airplane (Grace Slick!), Big Brother and the Holding Company (Joplin!), The Pretenders (Chrissie Hynde!), Odetta. The trailer park depressed her more in the mornings when all the speed bumps forced her to see too much, and she'd hate herself for being there, then break it off before relenting a week later and going back. It was a good stereo. And good pot. Was he still in there? Were his grandchildren? He had congratulated her on getting out of town via her scholarship to Belmont University, told her she'd know where to find him. She stayed for her Master's, worked in Nashville bars and restaurants, waited for a break (alongside her coworkers), got a couple jobs as a backup singer on Music City Row, sang in clubs (even the airport location of Tootsies Orchid Lounge), left town way past the tipping point that is the moment one learns The Business is a force of nature, applied for full-time/temporary teaching jobs and moved to Wisconsin where she did, on occasion, find value in teaching young women to remove that breathy, wispy, whiny timbre coming from the backs of their throats.

"Your mother's been good to me. I shouldn't be surprised, but after being gone so long and popping up one day without a dollar to my name? It's nice when people can surprise you, isn't it? I've been trying to surprise her too. I put her in a low-flush toilet and a new stainless steel kitchen sink with some flexible P-trap piping. And that day she saved my life? She came over with a pot of leftover beans and found me passed out on the floor."

"She told me."

"She called 911 and they took me to the emergency room. Turns out I'd messed myself while I was passed out, a bile as yellow as that line on the side of the road there, which is why I think it's my liver. It's made me appreciate the little time I've got left. Say you're hungry?"

"No," she said, loudly enough for Trina to jump, but he was slowing now past the Waffle House, past a group of smokers sitting outside around a table they'd moved there, one of them pointing to the sky. Behind them, the second 'n' of the Win -Dixie sign was burned out, just as it was at Christmas. She hadn't eaten all day and wasn't hungry.

"Looks like they're jam-packed, honey. It's kind of trendy these days for some reason. I'll tell you the worse thing I've done lately though."

"Please don't."

"Before I came here, I rented a little place in North Carolina, raising chickens, tending a garden, staying out of trouble, then one evening about dinner time, I shot my neighbor's dog with a .45 caliber handgun."

Maria tapped his shoulder so he'd face her, then shouted so he'd hear. "You shot your neighbor's dog?"

"He'd killed my two best laying-hens. After he killed Queenie, I went to my neighbor and warned him, said if that dog kills another chicken, I'm going to shoot him. He killed another one, and I shot him. We had a falling-out then. He came over and yelled at me, said it was his little girl's dog, this sweet little girl used to come over and talk to me and pet my chickens. I figured he was about to kill me. He came back the next day and apologized for yelling, and I told him I was sorry too—I shouldn't have done it like that. I told him the Lord forgave me, and I hoped he would too. Then he told me he'd like to have that dog's collar back—a shock collar that wasn't working that cost him twenty dollars. I went back to the woods where I'd put the dog out and got his collar. He never apologized for my dead chickens. I counted on those eggs."

Maria stared at this man to see if anything in his face resembled hers. No. He was a stranger when she met him and he would remain one as soon as she could leave, or as soon as he stole whatever he was going to steal from her mother and disappeared again.

"But I'll tell you something else I did that kind of evened things out," he said.

At the edge of an open field, a billboard announced an Olive Garden coming soon. They passed a pharmacy, a dollar store, another pharmacy, an auto parts store, another pharmacy.

"Couple months ago, I found a sick vulture in the woods—poor little thing was standing inside a rotten log, too weak to move. Must've had a hurt wing, so I went to my truck and got Trina's dog crate—one I'd used to carry her to the vet for her checkup, and I put that vulture in it and brought him home and put him inside the empty chicken pen your Uncle Mark built. Named him Claude after this preacher I knew. On the way home, I scooped up some roadkill and threw that in there with him—an old opossum that took a few days to start stinking good enough to arouse Claude's appetite—your mother noticed it about the same time."

They passed the forty-acre field Maria knew in her childhood as an alligator farm owned by a previous mayor that also held three bomb shelters built in the 1950s that were (according to rumor) stocked with beans, board games, and Bibles. Rows of enormous oaks, 500 years old, with sprawling limbs propped on cinderblocks, had survived again, but the ground between them held so many moss-coated limbs it looked like the Confederate army was there, lying dead.

"I scooped up roadkill for a few weeks. Fed him a porcupine once, which was interesting to watch him eat that, and he started gaining weight and looking better, and one day I opened the door for him and he walked right out and took off, pretty as you please." He bent over his steering wheel and looked into the sky. "Sometimes, I see him up there watching me."

He passed the church on the right with a stained-glass window blown out, then crossed three creeks and turned onto the dirt road toward home. Maria lowered her window and felt warm wind on her face. When was the last time she felt warm wind? The pines thickened on both sides as the road narrowed, and around the next curve, a blown-over trailer came into view, half-concealed by trees and vegetation.

"There's my house," he said. "Looks better upside down."

Behind the trailer, scattered through another grove of trees and bushes sat a collection of riding lawnmowers in various stages of decay, some missing hoods and wheels. On the seat of one mower, two black cats lifted their heads.

"There's Leon and Redbone. I'm glad they made it. I thought I was going to take over your Uncle Mark's small engine repair business, but my eyes are going, and I can't see well enough to fix anything. Last week, I got my .12 gauge and tried to kill a rattlesnake that was curled up close to my feet so it wouldn't get the cats, and I missed it three times. They say the snakes are bad this year."

Past the trailer, the dirt-road dead-ended at her mother's house, her childhood home, a fully intact roof lying on the ground in front of it, as if it was covering a buried home. The house remained intact. The rafters that held the roof were visible, fully prepared to hold the roof if only some giant hand could reach down and drop it back in place.

"Holy shit," Maria said.

"May the Lord's mercy be upon us and grant us peace," her father said.

On the far side of the roof, Maria spotted her mother squatting in her flowerbed. She wore her gardening hat and gloves, Toto lying beside her in the dirt. She stood with a handful of weeds and turned at the sound of the approaching car and waved a trowel toward Maria, who sprang from the car and ran toward her mother while Toto barked and wagged her tail. She hugged her mother tightly, and her mother hugged back without releasing the weeds or trowel.

"I guess y'all are acquainted now. Isn't your father nice?"

"Here we are," he said. "Together at last."

Maria leaned against the house. She closed her eyes, waiting for a dizzy spell to pass.

"I was just thinking about you," May said. "Thinking how hard I worked to keep a roof over our heads, and now look." May pointed at the roof on the ground and laughed.

"But what a nice skylight it is," Maria's father said, and laughed. "When God closes a door, he opens a roof."

"Are you hungry?" May said. "Maynard, you should whip us up something."

Maynard? Her father's name was *Maynard?* She put a hand on each side of her eyes.

"I sure will," he said. "I'll go to Winn-Dixie and get something nice in honor of our daughter coming home. Are you a wine drinker, Maria? Your mother's partial to the red zinfandels, but I'll get whatever you like."

Since when did her mother drink wine?

"Use my credit card," May said.

"I appreciate your generosity more than you can know," he said.

"You're giving him your credit card?" Maria said.

"You know what goes good with red zins?" Maynard said. "That kale salad with grapes and walnuts and feta cheese they have in the deli."

Maria felt the ground tilt, the sky curve. "I have to lie down," she said. She went to her childhood bedroom and lay on a bed littered with leaves. She looked at the sky, clouds planted there in the shapes of swollen brains and gargoyles and laughing demons. Then woke in the dark to a soft chant from the Cistercian Monks of Stift Heiligenkreuz. From beneath her pillow. Her phone. The sky was littered now with stars dripping salt through the warm night air. The salt fell through the open roof and offered a second skin. The stars were chanting. Her phone said Marty.

She whispered a soft and sleepy hey and he answered with a matching kind of sleepiness, as if he too had traveled a great distance, or had been awake a long time, worried, and then he was asking why she hadn't replied to any of his texts and was she okay, and how was her mom, and what about her father, the stranger—what was he like?

"I should've come with you," he said. "I'll come now."

She held her phone toward the stars, so he could hear them. From some direction she couldn't ascertain came the sound of water, like a river walking toward her. Crickets rode the river to her bedside, stood on their hind legs and faced her, waiting for her signal, which she issued telepathically. Behind them, tree frogs struck kettle drums. The chanting started up again, from above this time, from inside strands of moss that pulled her toward a deeper sleep, where she saw a circle of wounded birds roosting on her bed, eyes open.

"Hello?" he said. "You there?"

When she woke again, soft light drizzled through the roof. The birds were outside now, and loud, throats full of some startling news. The sheets were damp from sweat or rain. Over her face, some other face hovered now. A warm palm touched her cheek and it felt good. Maria wanted the palm to linger there while she kept her eyes closed. She smelled coffee and bacon dripping from the sky, and a man's voice came singing among the smells, some soft and melodic ballad with an Irish lilt surprisingly pitch-perfect and lovely. Her mother's palm tested her other cheek, then her forehead and the singing continued.

"Here we go with the wreck of Edmund Fitzgerald," May said. "He loves to sing this while he cooks. Not bad, huh?"

When Maria cracked her eyes open, she saw a big black vulture perched on the rafters, its wings spread as wide as Maria's body was long, drying its feathers. The blue sky beyond it looked bluer because of the bird's blackness. A wingspan wide enough to wrap her up and keep her warm. Its red-capped wrinkled head bald except for three black hairs sticking up, red nostrils big enough to hold shotgun shells, a prehistoric-looking wild creature related to the pterodactyl come from the deepest corner of a swamp.

The singing man stopped singing and said, "Good morning, Claude, you sweet son of a bitch you." Then the singing resumed. Such wonderfully elongated vowels delivered in steadily sustained notes and crisp diction: "Does anyone know where the love of God goes, when the waves turn the minutes to hours?" May leaned closer, touched both of Maria's cheeks at once and whispered something about the pleasant light.

May's face looked like a young mother pulling the fever out of her sick child. Beyond her, perched on the rafters, Claude's wings remained spread. He lowered his bald head toward Maria, who was levitating now (wasn't she?) toward his black and unblinking eyes, in the center of which she glimpsed something so beautiful and honest that she prayed for Marty to hurry home so Claude could heal him too.

What Doesn't Kill Us Makes Us Stranger

Monday morning at dialysis, nurse Gretchen brought me an extra blanket so I wouldn't freeze to death in that room they had to keep so cold, then Hope, the blue-eyed therapy dog, made her rounds and put her chin in my lap while I watched Joan Crawford and Bette Davis on TCM, and at some point that song came through the speakers that meant a baby had just been born, which made everybody smile for a second, and when my three hours were up, I said, "Do I have to leave?" and nurse Gretchen said, "Go home." She pointed to the sign above the door: *Don't live to eat, eat to live!* She said, "Clarissa—try eating *Brazil* nuts instead of *do*nuts," and I said, "Shit. How many Brazil nuts does it take to make a meal?" She said she wouldn't know; she'd never had one. Which is some people's luck.

They didn't like me to drive afterwards, but I performed a mind-trick that worked: I summoned my dead grandmother to ride shotgun so she could keep me awake. She said, "You better *open* your eyes. You better hold it together for those two grandbabies who have nobody else in this world to depend on. Remember how *I* held it together while I was raising you up and had nobody else? You think *I* had any help?" And she carried me home like that.

But today, another January day below zero degrees deep in the heart of another Wisconsin winter with more clouds pressing down, I only made it as far as the driveway. When I stepped from the car, I toppled face-first to the concrete. I don't know how long I lay there before my neighbor showed up. I'd never spoken to him, but for three years I'd seen him making his laps around the neighborhood, eyes fixed on the ground, moving slow and steady, younger than me. In the summer, if I saw him when I checked my mail or watered my petunias, I'd try to say hello, but he never looked at me. He wouldn't have looked if I'd stepped in front of him and did a naked dance and waved both arms over my head. But here he was, helping me up, keeping me steady while I found my key and opened the door, helping me inside and out of my coat and to the couch, moving the girls' stuffed animals and computers.

I said, "Excuse the mess, I don't have—thank you." I lay on the couch and closed my eyes, said, "I have to sleep now."

He stood over me. Said his name was Marty. Said, "Is there someone I can call?"

Like his voice was coming through water. Like he was bent over with his hands behind his back, which reminded me how Henry, my dead husband, used to knock gently on my forehead to wake me some mornings and ask was there anybody home in there, then he'd laugh, which made me chuckle now, like I was in a good dream.

"No," I said. "Nobody's home. Just pass me that blanket."

"Can I ask," he said, "if you don't mind. Can I ask what's going on?"

"I'm dying, honey. You are too. That blanket back of the chair there."

I opened my eyes and saw him looking at my pictures of Henry and my son Reggie and the grandbabies, and the two paintings my grandmother, who never had an art class in her life, painted of the wild horses running on the Cumberland

Island beach, next to some other photos of south Georgia close to where I grew up.

"That afghan," I said.

"My grandmother made it when I was a baby, sixty years ago."

He said, "Is that Cumberland Island?"

My eyes were closed, but I saw it. "That's right."

"Beautiful place," he said.

Another time, I would've asked him how he knew, but I had to sleep, rest up for all I had ahead of me: pick up my grandbabies from school, get their supper and wash some clothes and pay some bills and make their lunches for the next day and get some better sleep and wake them up and get them off to school and take myself to work where I'd work all day for the wicked witch of the Midwest, then pick up the girls and take them by the jail to visit their father, get their supper and get them bathed and into bed and back up and off to school and take myself back to dialysis.

"Right behind you," I said. "That afghan."

He went to the kitchen. Said he was writing down his name and number in case I needed a ride to the emergency room. Lived a block away. Marty something.

"Smells good in here," he said.

I'd put on a roast early that morning before I got the girls up, fixed most of it late Sunday night, peeled and chopped potatoes, carrots, garlic, onions, mushrooms, left it in the fridge over night to marinate with a half-bottle of dark beer, Worcestershire, smoked paprika, thyme, cayenne, six drops of smoke, then put it on in the morning, ready by 6 p.m.

He said, "Let me know if you need anything."

"That blanket," I whispered, but he was gone.

How much sleep does it take to feel rested without being dead? I wouldn't know. My phone woke me at 2:59, and I was glad—it gave me fifteen minutes to pick up the girls. It was Jill, my sister, calling from Georgia, so I didn't answer. She only called to complain about whatever petty thing was going wrong in her life, so she'd call again soon. I got up and held the wall while a dizzy spell washed over me, prayed I wouldn't pass out. Found my shoes. Scarf. Coat. Gloves. Hat. Purse. Keys. Stepped into the kind of cold that greeted me like an army of angry wasps. The girls told me they could ride the bus if it made things easier, but I said no, it was too cold to walk two blocks from the corner. Even when the weather was good, I didn't want them walking. There were too many mean drivers zooming across this little town, and I didn't trust any of them.

Grandma said, "Buckle up. Hold it together. You know how long I went without sleep when I was raising you up? Thirteen years. Did you ever notice? You never noticed. You know why you never noticed? Because I never complained, did I? You ever hear me complain? No, you didn't. You know why? Because I never did."

I was on the waiting list for a new kidney. My son Reggie had offered to give me one, but I told him *shut up*. He needed to be healthy for his girls longer than I did. Jill mentioned it once years ago, saying if only she had the money for a plane ticket, etc., but I didn't want her kidney. I wanted a kidney from a dying person. I said, "When you're dying, give me a call."

I parked as close as I could so my grandbabies wouldn't have to walk as far, but it was far enough to set their teeth to chattering. They needed new coats. Tuesday—no, there wasn't time Tuesday, but Wednesday after dialysis, I would use my credit card and buy them better coats.

Alyx, my third grader, sat in the front, face scowling at the cold. She said, "I hate my teachers and I hate this school and I hate this place."

Alicia, my first grader, said, "She punched this dumbass boy square in the nose. This boy came up to her and said the

President was going to put us on a boat and send us back to Mexico. She said shut up and he said make me, then she punched him square in the damn nose. Bled all over his white shirt. The teacher sent her to the principal who's going to call you for a meeting."

"A boat to Mexico?" I said. We're not even—"

"I *told* you," Alicia said. "He's a dumbass *boy*."

Alyx stared out her window. There wasn't much to see but snow—dirty snow on the curb, snow across the yards and snow on the roofs. "A boat to Mexico," I repeated. "That *is* a dumbass boy." I tried to think of how to cheer them up. I knew my pot roast wouldn't do it. I said, "Who wants ice cream?"

"Too damn cold for ice cream," Alicia said.

"We better get some donuts, then," I said.

I got a dozen glazed, one sourdough; promised them one before dinner, one after dinner. At home, they sat on the couch, ate their donuts while staring at their computers, each with headphones plugged in. Then the principal called, voice cold and flat, explained that Alyx had instigated a violent incident and could I meet tomorrow at 3:15, along with Alyx and a counselor.

"And what about the young gentleman who insulted my granddaughter?" I said. "Will he and his parents be joining us?"

"Not at this juncture," he said.

"Not at this juncture. Right. Yes, I'd be happy to meet."

I sat at the table with my checkbook and that box of donuts and a pen and notepad and looked through the bills to decide what to pay now and what to pay later. From most to least there was: the credit card, hospital, car payment, heating bill, car insurance, phone and internet. The house was paid for thanks to Henry—we'd put more money toward that while he was alive and paid it off after fifteen years, then threw ourselves a two-person party with champagne. He'd worked for twenty-nine years at Trane, moved up to shift supervisor, died at sixty-one, nine months before he was going to retire with a pension. Died in his sleep August 14, three years ago, after accusing my beans of giving him indigestion. Then Reggie came home from Afghanistan a different person, tried to find someone who would hire him, but no one would.

The credit card bill had the new water heater on it, a new car battery, and the girls' computers I got them for Christmas because they'd been saying they needed them for school, that every other child in the world had one. The heating bill was $320. I wrote that check and put it in an envelope. I took the girls their bowls of pot roast, scolded them to eat, gave them another donut. Made their lunches. While I cleaned the kitchen, Jill called again. I had no energy for her. It was all I could do to get the girls to close their computers and get a bath and into bed by 9 p.m.

From beneath her blankets, Alyx said, "Tomorrow's my turn to see Daddy."

"Right after we talk to your principal."

"My principal's a dumbass. You'll see."

"Probably so," I said. "Let's get some sleep anyway."

At 5 a.m., I came up out of another dream of falling through the same spot on an icy lake while nurse Gretchen stood on the shore holding a blanket, Hope sitting beside her. I made coffee. Ate a donut. Put in a load of clothes. Took out the load I'd left in the dryer and folded them. Ate another donut. Woke the girls. Put their cereal in front of them. Packed their lunches. Got them dressed and bundled them up and drove them to school through another gray and freezing day in this place where the sun was a stranger too.

Outside the school, I said, "I'll meet y'all outside the principal's office at 3:15. Let's see if we can all get through the day without punching anybody."

I watched their backs until they got inside. Then I drove to work, toward Ms. Schultz's house, the lady who, for three years, *I'd* been wanting to punch in the nose.

Grandma said, "Be nice. She's dying faster than you are."

But her problem was she didn't know it, so it didn't do her any good. She was ninety, in good shape from the neck down. From the neck up, she was in bad-enough shape to think her meanness made her smart. Some people's dementia turned them nice; hers made her mean. I would've rather changed the bedpans and cleaned the asses of any of my former clients than to spend a half-hour with Ms. Schultz.

My phone rang—Jill calling.

"Talk to your sister," Grandma said.

"Nope." At a red light, I looked into the car next to mine at a woman in her bulky coat, scarf and hat, holding her wheel with both gloved hands, looking straight ahead like a zombie facing the all-day job she must've dreaded going to as much as I dreaded going to mine.

Grandma said, "Damn. That lady reminds me of me. Turn on the radio."

In the five seconds before I could turn it off again, I heard too much about some politician eager to take away my health insurance. Ms. Schultz loved his stupid ass. She thought she voted for him, but she didn't. When I drove her to vote on November 5, I pulled up to the handicapped spot, and when the lady came out with the ballot, Ms. Schultz asked me to fill it out. I read the choices and filled in the bubbles next to the names she *didn't* want. Then the lady handed me the *I Voted!* sticker, and I pressed it onto Ms. Schultz's collar. She was so proud of herself she suggested we drive through the DQ on the way home, get a couple Blizzards, her treat, she said, and she gave me a ten-dollar bill and made me count back the change.

"She's had a hard time," Grandma said. "Try to sympathize."

Her husband drank himself to death when he was six-ty-five, died on the morning of their fortieth wedding anniversary, a fact she liked to repeat. What took him so long, I don't know. Her daughter was in her third alco-hol-rehab place after losing custody of her three children to her ex-husband, who took them to California "to live with fruitcakes." Her son moved to Spain with his husband and never called. She'd outlived her friends, if she'd ever had any. I tried to think of all this while I drove through her nice neighborhood full of trees and big yards. I tried to remind myself that even rich people had problems, that everybody was suffering in some way.

"That's the spirit," Grandma said. "You think I had a self-ish bone in *my* body all those years I was sacrificing for you, when I could've moved to Hawaii and married a prince?"

"Shit," I said. "You never thought of going to Hawaii."

"That's what I'm saying," she said. "I couldn't think of myself for one second. Get in there and give that old bitch a smile."

I walked in and shouted good morning because she was facing her news-blaring TV, and before I could take off my coat, she said, "It's 8:05, Clarissa; there are plenty of people who would be grateful to show up on time."

All day, I wondered how I could get away with killing her. My job was to clean, make her lunch and tea, deliver her pills on a tray, take her to the grocery store on Senior Morning Wednesdays. Today, I got to work so I could avoid her: swiped my dust cloth around every room, moved her miniature lighthouses so she'd think I'd gotten between them, then pushed her heavy vacuum cleaner across her thick shag carpet, swept and mopped her kitchen, cleaned her toilets. She said but wouldn't a fire be nice? I carried in wood from the garage and made a fire, went back for another load so I could keep feeding it, all while the dumbass loud mouths from her news show shouted dumbass things between loud commercials. She refused to wear her hearing aids unless she was going out because what was the point of hearing *me*?

After she ate the pimiento cheese sandwich I cut into triangles, she said, "But wouldn't some ice cream be good?" so I gave her a big portion so it would knock her out. And soon after she finished clanking her bowl to scrape up every tiny little morsel, she started snoring. I muted the TV, then sat in the chair next to her and closed my eyes. A minute later, she was knocking my leg with her cane, shouting in German like she did when she got upset.

I said, "What the hell's wrong with you?"

In English, she said, "It's snowing, Clarissa!"

I looked out—fat flakes fell in big chunks, but it hadn't been falling long.

"The city will fine me if my sidewalks aren't shoveled," she said.

This *fine*—I happened to know because I'd gotten one last year—was handed out if you didn't shovel within twenty-four hours after it *stopped* snowing, not twenty-four seconds after it started. But I thought being outside in the freezing cold would prevent me from choking her. I put on my coat, scarves, hat, gloves, and shoes and went to shovel her corner lot, which meant two sidewalks, plus her driveway and walk. Heavy snow. I made two scoops and stopped for a breath. Two scoops and a breath. Then one scoop and a breath. I stayed out too long. Kept looking at the young man next door pushing his snowblower down his little strip of a sidewalk, ten feet away, some of it blowing into my face—looked at him in case he needed my permission to push his blower down Ms. Schultz's sidewalk. He ignored me. When I finally finished and went back in, I must've looked half-dead. Ms. Schultz said, "Oh, Clarissa, you look frozen. Add some wood to the fire and make us some warm tea."

My lips were too numb to move. I put a log on the fire, poked it, going slow so I could warm up. I made her tea decaf so she'd doze off. But I dozed off too. When I woke, she was staring at me. She said, "Clarissa, you were sleeping on the job."

I tried to reason with her, say something she might sympathize with. "Those grandbabies," I said. "They keep me up too late." She couldn't hear me. But I saw her looking at me softly, head cocked to the side, a new expression, like she was ready to trade confessions.

"Truth is," I said, speaking so loudly that it was *work*, "I'm taking dialysis three times a week, so it's wearing me down a little, but not enough to keep from working. And I *need* to work because of my grandbabies. I feel better on Tuesdays, Thursdays, Saturdays, and Sundays. And I'm high on the list to get a transplant as soon as somebody with a matching kidney dies. That's all I'm waiting for. When I get a new kidney, I'll work full-time."

Ms. Schultz said, "You poor old woman."

I didn't think the *old* was necessary, but at least she was on the verge of sympathy.

"You should've said something sooner," she said.

"I'll be better Thursday, after I rest up."

"Maybe you shouldn't come back at all, dear," she said.

"I'll be okay Thursday."

"You should hire someone to look after *you*," she said.

I laughed at this, imagining I could pay someone to serve me. "I'm okay," I said. "I just shoveled that sidewalk and driveway, so I'm a little tired."

"I have to insist, Clarissa. I don't want to be responsible for worsening your condition, and I can't put you in a position that might jeopardize my well-being. What if you fell asleep while the house was on fire? What if I went into cardiac arrest and needed you to call 911?"

"I'm okay. I can call 911 if I need to. I'm just a little extra tired today, but—"

"Hand me my purse. I'll settle up with you for this week, and you can go home early, get some rest. Sue will be here at three and can see about replacing you. She may want the extra shift herself. She's a very good worker, Sue is."

I stared at the woman's old face, her pouty lips, those cold blue eyes behind her glasses. I thought: here is the lady who whistles while leading you to the gas chamber.

She kept her purse beneath her chair so she'd know where it was. I had to get on one knee—like I was genuflecting for the Queen—just to pull it out, then I placed it on her lap. She handed me her checkbook, said, "Make it out to yourself for $60, and let me sign it."

She couldn't see well enough to write her own checks and couldn't hold a pen tightly enough. I was tempted to make it out for $600. Instead, I took two twenties from her purse, called it my severance package. I did this while she held the check up against her glasses to make sure I'd written $60. Then I put a book in her lap so she could sign it. I put her checkbook back in her purse and slid her purse back between her legs under her chair. She said, "Will you return this book to its proper place?" I returned the book to the coffee table in front of her. I put on my coat, gloves, scarf, hat, and shoes without a word. I did not punch her in the nose.

"Good luck," she said.

I lifted my middle finger to her back, then stepped from the house into the cold and snow, legs heavy as cypress stumps. It was coming down in thick sheets now, heavier than I'd ever seen. *Good luck*, I said, and laughed. Grandma said, "You done messed up now. You thought you could tell that woman you were feeling weak? *Never* tell the boss you're feeling weak."

I thought I'd seen an invitation to confide something.

"Buckle up," Grandma said. "What don't kill us, make us stranger."

Tomorrow, after dialysis, I'd look for another job. I got a small disability check every month, and I had a tiny bit in savings—enough for a couple weeks-worth of food, but I'd have to find something soon. Maybe I'd ask the principal if he had any openings. I had an hour before I saw him. What could I do with an hour? The snow fell thick and fast, and I had a corner lot too, so I knew I should shovel some now so it would be less heavy later, then gather up a little care package to take Reggie, a couple books he'd asked for, a notebook to write in.

Grandma said, "Better call the jail."

They had strict rules about visiting hours, which were 4-8 p.m. Tu/Th/Sat, twenty minutes per visit, only one child per visit, and only if you called first to get on the list. If you called and didn't show up, you lost visiting privileges for a month.

I got my phone out.

"Better wait 'till we get home." Grandma said. "*If* we get home."

I backed out of Ms. Schultz's driveway, turned my wipers on high, went slowly through her neighborhood toward the main road. The snow was sticking, piling up. Last winter, the mechanic who put a new battery in my '96 Corolla (190,000 miles) tried to sell me new tires. He said my tread was as bald as his head. I told him I'd wait. He'd said *good luck*.

Grandma said, "Better speed up. You're going to get us run over and killed."

I'd gotten in front of a city snowplow who was riding my ass, looking like he was ready to throw me to the curb.

My phone rang. Jill.

"Don't answer that. Look at the road."

I couldn't *see* the road.

"Better slow down."

I wouldn't tell Reggie I'd been fired. He had enough worries. His court date kept getting delayed because his appointed lawyer had quit and he was waiting for a new one. His last lawyer said he was looking at six months to six years, depending on the judge. I knew he smoked pot. I knew about his gun. When he came back from Afghanistan he couldn't sit still, and he couldn't be in public either. The pot relaxed him enough to leave the house and look for work. He didn't smoke around me or the girls. Then on November 6 is when he got the gun, which was the same morning we woke up and saw somebody had spray-painted our front door with the words "Go home!" Same door I'd been going through since 1985, when Henry and I bought the house. It was three months after we'd come here from Georgia to visit his aunt and uncle, which is when he saw that job at Trane and got it and worked his way up. I was glad Reggie had the gun. He kept it under his car seat when he went out, then kept it on a high shelf in his closet when he came home. He sat us at the kitchen table, told us about it, told us never to go inside his closet.

"Watch out, fool," Grandma said.

Some fool kid wearing shorts and a t-shirt decided to walk across the middle of the street, ignorant of crosswalks.

"Maybe *he's* got a matching kidney," she said.

Then in early December, a K-9 unit pulled Reggie over for supposedly rolling through a four-way stop, claimed he had enough pot for a distribution charge, plus the unregistered handgun, which somehow added up to a six-year max. Waiting for his court date was killing him. He wanted to get it over with, let his girls know how soon he'd be back. All I could do was bring them to visit and hold it together myself when I was in front of him so he'd worry less. He'd been trying, God knows. When he graduated from the state college in 2011, he owed $25,000 in student loans. He worked two jobs for a year after college, but it wasn't enough and then had a two-year-old girl and another on the way, both with this woman whose name I refuse to mention, and this Marine recruiter kept calling, saying the GI Bill would pay off his loans after his four years, which was not the whole truth. Six months after he came home, that woman disappeared and left him with two little girls she said she'd never wanted. He and the girls moved in with me. For a couple months, he drove me to dialysis and picked me up when it was over, then saw about supper. He had applications in all over town, and he was fighting to hold it together, even enrolled in a yoga course and started dating the teacher who said *he* should be the teacher. He kept telling us everything would be fine, and I could tell by the way his girls looked at him that they believed him. He told them every Tuesday, Thursday, and Saturday, and they still believed him. But the waiting was wearing on them too. The waiting was killing us.

At a red light I watched the heavy snow coming down and piling up and knew the shoveling would be difficult, so I closed my eyes for a second. A car horn woke me.

"Let's go," Grandma said. "Pay attention."

After I pulled into my garage, I didn't even go inside. I grabbed the shovel and started clearing a path as wide as the car so I could get out and back in again. When I looked over to my sidewalk, my neighbor Marty was there, clearing it away like he was on the Olympic snow-shoveling team. I walked over to thank him, snot dripping from my nose.

He said, "I'll be back later—looks like ten more inches is on the way." Then he was off, shovel over his shoulder, limping back toward his house, a sight that made me want to cry because I thought he'd hurt his back by shoveling too much too fast, just for me. If he could wait long enough for me to find the time, I'd make him a cake, tell him to share it with his wife, who looked like she could put on a pound or two.

After I went inside and took off my coat, gloves, scarf, hat, and boots, I collected Reggie's things, then I called the jail to tell them we were coming at 4 p.m. I put the morning's wash in the dryer, washed the breakfast dishes, sat on the couch for just one minute. My phone woke me at 2:59. My first thought was that I was late to the principal's office, so I answered fast without looking.

"Clarissa." It was Jill. "Listen," she said. "I have to talk to you."

I stood too quickly, held the wall while a dizzy spell washed over me.

"I need you to come home," she said. "You and the girls."

"I can't talk now," I said. "I've got to—"

"I tried to call you yesterday when I found out. I—"

"Can't find my damn gloves," I said.

"They're telling me six months to a year."

"Can't find my damn scarf either."

"It came back," she said. "Spread to my pancreas."

I went to the garage without my coat or gloves or hat. The school wasn't far.

"I've got to go to the damn principal's office," I said. "You believe that?"

"My kidneys are okay, Clarissa. I need you and the girls to come home."

I turned my wipers on high and moved slowly through the falling snow.

"Are you hearing me?" she said.

"No," I said. "I'm not hearing you. I'm driving through a damned blizzard and it's minus 20 damn degrees and this old bitch just fired me and I've got to go to the damned principal's office because Alyx punched a dumbass kid whose damned parents won't be there, then we're going to the jail to see Reggie for twenty minutes, which is all we get. *Twenty minutes.*"

Grandma said, "I hope these other drivers can see you're on the phone!"

I couldn't tell where the road stopped and the sky started because the sky and the road were the same color. All around my periphery was the same color too, big as an ocean.

"You and the girls come live with me," Jill said. "I want you to have my house."

"I'll call you later," I said. "I can't even—"

I heard the body—like a bag of bones and bricks—hit my car before I saw it. Then the body was rolling up the hood and up the windshield, not stopping until it reached eye-level, then it paused and hovered long enough to reveal two inches of flesh between shirt and pants, a hairless little belly button belonging to a child. The body rolled back down. Rolled so slowly I saw all the way back to a summer day when Reggie rolled down a country hill, screaming with joy until he slowed to a stop in a patch of wildflowers. But this body fell off the hood like it had fallen off a mountain, then disappeared.

My hands didn't know what to do. Nothing was moving but the snow, which kept coming down. A kid lying in the street. Then sitting. Then scooting backwards by the seat of his pants, one leg bent, one leg straight, crawling backwards toward the curb like a hurt crab.

Grandma said, "Oh hell, honey. Hold on, now. Everybody just hold on."

Even while I watched him reach the curb and crawl up the snowbank and sit on top of it and stare ahead in a frozen trance—even then, my mind wouldn't tell my hands what to do.

Grandma said, "Get out there and see about him, honey. I'll wait in the car." One person, then another, came running toward the child.

Grandma said, "Put the car in park and turn it off."

I did this. I unfastened my belt. People had huddled around the child.

The wasps stung my face. I held to my car fender like a guardrail, then stepped around to the hood, felt it dip in the middle where the body had made a dent.

Two people were talking on their phones, smoke coming out of their mouths, looking down the street toward the sound I recognized as a siren. I couldn't see the child. Couldn't get to the child. Had anyone called the child's mother? Somebody needed to. I imagined getting that same call and looked for a place to vomit. Wasps were stinging my lips and face. Falling snow piled on my head and shoulders. I wanted to see the child, but there were too many bodies between us. The siren came closer. I said, to no one, "I have to go to the principal's office."

The siren stopped beside my head. People pointed. Cleared a path. The EMTs rushed forward, carrying a toolbox, a stretcher. Two cops followed. People were pointing at me.

The EMTs disappeared into the crowd and the crowd closed around them.

The cops were walking toward me. One stepped up and removed a pen, smoke coming out of his mouth, very tired-looking himself, like he hated this job he'd been working too many years in the kind of cold that was locked inside him now. A familiar face. Had I seen his face at the jail, or a face like his? His brother's face?

"I have to get my girls," I told him, or tried to, but my lips weren't working. He said something into the walkie-talkie fastened to his shoulder, then a woman said 10-4.

"We have to see Reggie for twenty minutes at four," I said, but my lips weren't working.

The other cop was in the road, waving cars around us, trying to get people moving, but they were busy looking, trying to find someone they could blame.

The woman cop wrapped a blanket around me and hugged it tight. The man cop said, "Have you been drinking? Were you texting?"

The woman said, "What's your name, honey?"

I tried to say, "Somebody needs to call his mother."

"What's your name?" the woman said. "Can you tell us that? And your address?"

"I have to see the principal," I said, or tried to.

"Tell me what happened," she said.

"Jill said come home," I tried to say. "My girls."

"Let's sit inside my car and get warm," the woman said.

She held the door open and I sat inside and she closed the door and went around and got in behind the wheel, and I hugged the blanket and waited to get warm.

"You're okay now," the woman said. "Just tell me what happened."

"Jill said come home," I said.

The woman looked at me like I didn't know where home was.

"Okay," the woman said. "Let's just wait—"

"It's in her pancreas," I said.

She got on her radio and called somebody.

"Call Jill," I said. "She'll tell you. Jill's my sister."

I waited. The snow-colored sky bled into the snow-covered ground.

Jill said come home. And I waited.

Reunions, Atrocious Manners, the Atlanta Airport

I didn't feel like going, but I went, and by the time I got there it was dark and everyone was poolside beneath tiki torches with flames bent sideways from the ocean wind, waves thundering on rocks, and all the faces were older now and hanging low because Blake was dead and therefore wasn't coming. Trip Champion (his real name!), my old classmate, the organizer, sent a group text hours earlier saying Blake had (and here's a warning about the mention of suicide) killed himself. Just last night at the same hotel where our 20th high school reunion was taking place. Unbelievable. A heavy gut punch, even for me, someone who didn't like him much, though I liked him more than I liked the others. If there had had been a "least likely to kill oneself," superlative, Blake would've gotten it. I could've won *most likely*. Blake never sulked the way I sulked. I was a valedictorian-level sulker—moody, angry, most likely to take a swing at someone like Trip Champion. Blake was a rich physician with a beautiful wife and two daughters ages five and seven, lived in New Orleans, played jazz piano on weekends. Trip's text said he'd understand if no one felt like attending, but *he'd* be there to offer support, to make it a life-celebration, which is what Blake would want, etc. So I thought of not going. Then I went.

Then thought immediately of leaving. When the invitation came, I'd ripped it up, pieced it back together, booked a flight, canceled, rebooked, then flew 1,000 miles from Wisconsin to northern Florida to see the fifteen classmates I'd known for two years twenty years ago at the private high school my mom put me in when I got expelled from the public school for urinating on a teacher's desk. And for fighting. And for stashing weed and liquor in my locker. My probation officer told my mom a new environment might help, so she took out a loan, said I'd be driving a half-hour to attend a college-prep private academy where I might, if nothing else, learn some manners. I didn't learn much. But here I was, ready to make amends. I wanted to tell them I'd quit drinking. I wanted to be tagged in a group photo and show it to Maria as proof that I was finally over all the silly shit I kept dreaming about. They were more mature now too, certainly, so I hoped they'd be quick to forgive me, to say I'd changed. *I'd* matured so much—hair loss, weight gain, bifocals—I feared I'd have to introduce myself.

I moved toward the small group huddled near the diving board with Jill Christianson in the center of them, looking tan and fit, long hair, windblown, everyone holding drinks in real glasses. Jill declined my senior prom invitation because of Blake, whom I knew she was dating. But I'd asked her anyway, a dick move I wanted to apologize for.

The millionaire Jill married, the father of her four (or nine?) perfect children (according to her social media brags), looked handsomely supportive, tan arm around her shoulders, and next to him stood George Shumate, who threw a New Year's Eve party he didn't invite me to (which didn't matter now), and next to him his tan wife wore a strapless black dress, and next to her was tie-wearing, thick-haired, bank-inheriting Trip, who was a major player among local leaders promoting tourism when he wasn't skiing in the Alps or surfing in Maui, according to his brags. It was Trip who first put 'Wal' in front of my name, Marty, as in, *What's up, Walmarty?* Because I worked at Walmart nights and weekends, the only one in the school who needed a job to help a single mom, apparently, which led me, one morning when the nickname sounded cruelest, to break his jaw for him. There was no spouse on his shoulder, so maybe he was alone, and when we made eye contact, there was something sad and forgiving there, so I turned my eyes to Jill, who tilted her head and said, "How are *you*?" so sincerely it threw me off guard.

"Terrible," I said.

"I can't believe it," she said.

Trip looked at me, said, "Did *you* have any idea? Did he ever—"

"No," I said, flattered that Trip would think I'd have access to Blake's inner life, that he might be remembering me as a popular kid Blake would trust with intimate info.

"How'd he do it?" I said. Surely I wasn't the first to ask.

Trip looked toward the top floor of the five-floor hotel. "He checked into a suite last night, wrote an email to his wife and daughters, then hung himself."

My first thought (the wrong one) was wondering what the ocean-view rooms cost. My second thought was I felt sorry for the hotel worker who found him. But then, yes, of course, his poor devastated wife and poor daughters and poor friends. It was upsetting.

"That's upsetting," I said.

"I can't believe it," Jill said again.

"Did anyone see the email?" I said.

I was full of insensitive questions. But wouldn't a reason be nice? Wasn't the *why* of it what we wanted? No one said anything. We had what DJ's called dead air.

On graduation night, Blake and Jill rented a beach house, and the entire class went skinny-dipping, following Blake, the first to strip and sprint into the ocean. Afterward (why did I remember this stupid thing?), with all of us still naked on the beach, I made a drunken speech declaring my love for every classmate and expressed my earnest wish that we would remain lifelong friends. That summer, I worked two jobs and never saw the others, then everyone dispersed for college while I lived with Mom and sulked around the community college for the three years it took me to get a nursing degree. When others came home over summers and breaks, I kept working, kept sulking, gave up on getting in touch.

Jill's handsome spouse changed the subject. Tall guy in a red polo tucked into black shorts, stylish glasses, nice teeth, sandals. He said, "What do *you* do for a living?" Meaning me. *This* was an insensitive question. My answer would be an instant judgment on my gross value, my net worth, my intelligence.

"Information systems for NASA," I said. They kept staring. "Not really. I was a travel nurse for awhile, moving around the country, which was hard, never staying in one place long enough to establish—you know—which has been a problem with me anyway, really, since my Dad split when I was two and left me alone with my mom, which was hard, and made me too angry while I was growing up, then I got fired over this DNR-thing involving this family in Idaho who wanted to go against their daughter's wishes; I mean, how long should you keep a zombie plugged in, you know? Then I moved home for a bit, met Maria, my wife, then six years ago moved with her to Wisconsin for her job—she's a music professor at a state university there. It was her idea that I come to this reunion because I keep dreaming about high school, which, I know, get over it already, right? Anyway, I work third shift now at a hospital in Environmental Services, which was nice at first because of the quiet nights, but the loud ventilators and moans from patients and beeping machines are wearing on me, and the nurses and doctors ignore me, but they're all tired too. Maybe Blake's job as a doctor is what did him in, I could see how." I'd said too much too quickly. We had a pause.

Jill's spouse filled it. "Wisconsin?" he said, like *Pluto?*

"I tried to get as far away as possible," I said, a joke that didn't land.

"You haven't changed," George said. "You're still an asshole."

"Pardon him," his pretty spouse said. "He's a psychiatrist, always on duty."

I hadn't meant to insult anyone. I was here to make amends.

"We're having a hard time right now," George said.

I heard the 'we' as *them*, excluding *me*, which—okay, but still.

"I can't believe it," Jill said, off with a story about the time they saw U2 in Miami, followed by scuba diving in the Keys, the greatest time she ever had, she said, right in front of her husband, and she sobbed. Then Trip told of a time he and Blake road-tripped to Mexico, and *he* started crying.

"He invited me to his house once," I said.

George stared at me coldly, like, *That's your best Blake story?*

"For a study group," I said. "For the final exam in Anatomy, which I was failing, which meant I wouldn't graduate, so Blake invited me over to study. Asked me to come early so I could play his Steinway Grand because he knew I spent lunch periods playing that old piano in the practice room." I didn't reveal that this particular night was among my best memories for the way Blake's Steinway responded to my fingers while I played the Beethoven I'd taught myself on my Walmart-bought plastic-keyed Casio, and for how the sun slanted through the windows of that large room and spread across the hardwood floors, and for how Blake left me alone for a half-hour then returned to hear the last notes of "Fur Elise," then put his hand on my shoulder and said, with feeling, "Sounds good."

"He was so kind," Jill said, and tucked her hair behind an ear, which the wind undid.

"I cheated like hell on that exam," I said, hoping *this* would get a laugh. It didn't. I'd kept a piece of folded paper beneath the test to see the names of bones and muscles, ligaments, arteries, blood vessels, the four systems of the body, the chambers of the heart. "I stole a laughing Buddha bust from him that night," I said. "Lifted it from a bookshelf and stuffed it in my backpack. I was going to apologize to him about that."

"This isn't about you," said George, the psychiatrist.

Yes. I knew. Of course.

"Of course," I said. "But *did* anyone see Blake's email to his wife? I wonder what—"

"Excuse me," George said, and walked to the shallow end of the pool and put his arm around Chrissy O'Connor, who was talking to Jim Carter, who put a hand on George's shoulder. Chrissy rejected my senior prom invitation too, blaming it on her father, who said he didn't know my family and didn't like that I'd lost my driver's license from a DUI and then got caught driving with a suspended license. I hoped Chrissy was as happy now as her posts portrayed, living a wealthy life in Barcelona, selling real estate, showing off her fluent Spanish.

"I quit drinking," I said to the group that remained.

"Not me," said Jill's spouse, who believed he'd get another. Someone else said *me too* and others said they needed a bathroom, then I was alone with Jill, who'd drunk too much.

She looked at me with her wet sad eyes, then hugged me. Her perfume filled my head with a memory of a warm spring day when I was alone and didn't want to be.

She said, "Listen. Don't ever go and do what Blake did without first checking with me first, okay?" She kissed my cheek. Then walked away. I stood there, alone again. Then slipped into the hotel lobby, then to the parking lot, then drove the half-hour home, to Mom's house, sulking for old times sake rather than calling Maria because she'd say, "How'd it go?" and I'd have to tell her about Blake, which *was* upsetting, and that I wish I hadn't gone at all, and she'd tell me, again, that I should talk to someone. And I'd say sure, right, but not right now.

Once home, I went to my old room, too awake, still on my third-shift schedule. I Googled the cost of Blake's ocean-view suite—$900. I replayed images that fell into dreams—Jill's kiss, *you're still an asshole*, Blake's face, a long email with words too small to see, *check with me first*, a Steinway Grand splashed with light, Jill's perfume, Blake's rope, a Buddha bust laughing from a landfill, *you haven't changed*, a mother snoring down the hall.

"Please behave yourself," Mom said while I drove us to the family reunion she'd been telling me about for three months, planned to coincide with my trip home, apparently, which I insisted was unnecessary.

"I'm thirty-eight years old," I said. "Do you think you need to say *behave yourself?*"

"You're grumpy. When you get grumpy, you lose your manners. It takes some men a long time to grow up. You'll get there one day."

"I am *not* grumpy," I said.

I was grumpy. I hadn't slept. For breakfast? A bruised banana. The August heat and humidity was a python-like assault on the lungs. Soon enough I was wiping my face with a paper towel while standing next to Uncle Stan and his cigarette and his barbecue smoker beneath an ancient oak tree in a park adjacent to the church that had helped convert me to atheism. Mom sat beside me, next to a table that held gallons of tea and red cups. Some cousins, aunts, and uncles came from distant places, meaning Alabama. I looked for my favorites—an aunt who loaned Mom my high school tuition money, an uncle who found and fixed a used car for me—but they were dead and therefore absent. Spanish moss blew from all the oaks like hung squirrels, and the warm wind was a relief. Uncle Stan talked of an approaching hurricane.

"I'll ride it out," he said. "I've got a twenty-thousand-watt generator and a 500 gallon gas tank that'll keep the house going for ten days if we lose power, air conditioner and all."

Stan owned a lawn care business called the Grounds Crew, though he was the sole operator, working twelve-hour days to make rich people's lawns as pretty as golf greens, which explained the large bandage on his left cheek, where he'd had a carcinoma removed.

Two younger cousins, Marie and Lynn, each carried a baby they introduced me to.

"Where's yours?" Lynn said.

"In a dumpster," I said.

"You're still not right in the head, are you?" she said, not joking.

"Such atrocious manners," Mom said.

Lynn was still a server at a nice restaurant at the Jacksonville Landing, still getting shitty tips and regular abuse, still married to Bill, an electrician, and Marie was still married to Mark, a carpenter, and still worked at a fancy hotel where just two days ago, she said, someone checked into an ocean-view suite just to hang himself.

"Must be nice," Stan said.

My face must've given me away because Marie said, "What? Did you know him?"

"Good friend of mine," I said, an exaggeration meant to give me attention, which was a childish move. "We went to high school together. I was at the hotel last night for a—does that room really go for $900 a night?"

"Closer to a grand with taxes," Marie said.

"Hey," shouted my uncle Vernon then, interrupting, rolling up in a wheelchair with an oxygen tank strapped to the back, tubes running to his nose.

"Who let you in?" he said, talking to me. One side of his face was bruised from a recent fall, the deep purple-black-red bruise blood thinners made worse, eye swollen shut as if he'd stepped repeatedly into a heavyweight's left hook. My mother's other remaining sibling, he once stood 6'5, but he was crumpled now, gasping in the humidity. I hated to see him looking so bad, this man who bailed me out of jail when I got my DUI, who gave me a complete set of Louis L'Amour hardbacks, who told me repeatedly to stiffen my posture, to remove my hat when entering a house, to stand when a lady entered a room, to carry a clean handkerchief.

Marie and Lynn wandered away, eager to avoid Vernon, who asked what it was I did these days. "For a living," he clarified. He'd spent his life using his body in his work—construction, brick mason, roofer—and now his body was paying him back. I told him what I did now after being fired for helping a terminal patient kill herself.

"Maybe you can help me later on," he said.

"What time?"

"Sign me up too," Stan said.

"Atrocious," Mom said.

In two more hours, after eating and repeating similar updates with others, Mom said her goodbyes, which took another hour, then she pushed her walker to the passenger side door of her Buick that I rushed ahead to open for her.

"Your manners have gone to hell," she said.

Had they? I folded up her walker and stowed it in the back and got in to drive us home.

"I'm sorry," I said, sounding like an infant.

"Maybe you should talk to a priest."

"Maybe so," I said, picturing such. With bourbon. With such honesty that the priest could share some shame too. I'd say, "Forgive me father, for I'm an asshole. I've tried to connect, and I have failed." I *had* tried. Why else attend such reunions? Why follow thousands of people on social media who don't follow back? Why make a post one week ago announcing a social media break so I could rediscover the real self that grew murky while trying to make an online self attractive? A half-hour after that post, I reactivated to see if anyone had liked it. Three people. Blake was one of them. Then I deactivated again.

When we got home, I took a nap, woke at 10 p.m., with Mom asleep. We didn't talk again until 7 a.m. on the way to the airport for my flight to Atlanta, where I'd layover three hours before flying to Minneapolis, where I'd layover two hours before flying home, ETA: 8 p.m.

She drove slowly, drifting across lanes. A tractor trailer full of dead pines unleashed a horn on her rear bumper.

"I can't see too good," she said. "Not even tractor trailers."

"Since when?"

"I'm having cataract surgery next month. I've told you that."

Had she? I wondered who would drive her to the surgery and who would take her home? Shouldn't I come back to help? Isn't that what a well-mannered son would do?

At the airport, car running, she said, "I raised you to be a gentleman. Give it a try."

I kissed her cheek, got my bag, watched her swerve toward a car that jutted around her.

At my gate, I popped a Valium to ease my flight anxiety, and in Atlanta, after a rocky flight, I took a second to cope with the mass of people rushing with bags that bumped against me in the over-packed tram. Someone was bare-footed. Someone else wore a wrestling mask. Someone else wore—I had to look twice—a snorkel! When I reached my gate and found a seat, I looked at all the open mouths around me, a germ-spewing horde of mouths opening around food, mouths moving into phones or toward each other, mouths of parents yelling at unruly children chasing each other as if they were in their living room. I tapped my hand on my leg and worried what bad behavior I'd be capable of should the smallest little thing go wrong.

Then the gate worker announced a delay. Then a ruckus. Some lunatic stormed up to the gate-worker and started throwing a tantrum, asking whether she had any fucking idea what important work was being delayed because of the airline's fucking incompetence. She didn't. In that case, he said, could she get her fucking superior on the fucking phone right away, please?

I wanted to punch the man on the gate-worker's behalf, on behalf of all workers who got abused by assholes. Then the asshole's phone went off, a work-related call, apparently because he answered, stepped away, started explaining the injustice he'd suffered. The whole scene shook me up. Across from our gate was a brightly lit headphone store, so I went there, found the nicest noise-canceling model available, put them on and said, *oh yes*, how nice to be so isolated. They cost more than my overdue car payment, so I put them back and walked to a coffee shop, waited a half-hour for a too-expensive coffee and returned to my gate, where I sat, ears exposed to the loud talkers around me I resented because I couldn't afford to shut them out.

A half-hour later, I walked across the thick carpet in first class enjoyed by rich fucks drinking Bloody Marys from real glasses. I moved toward 13E, a middle seat in Comfort, also costly, but what choice did I have when airlines gouged an ass my size? As I neared my aisle, I saw my seatmate at the window, a serene gentleman dressed in the type of white garb worn by practitioners of Tai Chi. He looked like a high-ranking monk (if ranking even exists among monks, which it wouldn't) saturated in wisdom, one who valued honest stories about the essence of despair and the desire to shed regret and cease the self-loathing your past self says you're stuck with, etc., which only just now I was being able to articulate (to myself, at least). He held a book I intended to ask him about. If he looked up to see me, he'd see a portrait of patience while I waited for the slow-ass people ahead of me to stuff their big-ass bags into overhead compartments. But he looked out the window, fixed in a reflection where forgiveness lived.

Someone sneezed, a man giggled, a baby screamed. The monk didn't flinch. Nor did he jump, as I jumped, at the flight attendant's amplified announcement: "We have a 285 on our hands, people. If you're not from Atlanta, you don't get that. We've got gridlock in the aisle, and a full flight, so please take your seats so we can stay an hour behind schedule." I slid past the vacant outside seat to the middle seat and lowered myself, holding the seat ahead of me for balance, then fell a half-foot, exhaled from the effort and said, "Good morning" to the monk, who pulled his headphones (identical to ones I'd tried on) up from his neck to cover his ears.

"I hear you," I said, raising my voice. "I wish I'd had some headphones like that during the class reunion and family reunion I just attended, on back-to-back days, if you can believe it, which has me asking how it is that so many of us—like my former classmate who seemed so happy—reach the ends of our ropes."

The monk stared ahead, concentrating, maybe misunderstanding. Did he know English?

"He hanged himself," I explained. "Poor guy."

The monk pushed his left headphone back.

"Sorry?" he said.

"Thank you. I mean, we were never *great* friends, and we'd lost touch for awhile, but it's still upsetting. He did it in a $1,000 hotel suite. Who rents a $1,000 suite to hang themselves? Just shows how we can't know the private suffering of others, right?" The monk lowered his head and sighed, and suddenly I felt guilty about the negativity I'd emitted into our shared space.

"I'm sorry," I said. "I've just emitted negativity into our shared space."

"Okay," he said, and lifted his book closer to his eyes to make it clear he'd prefer reading, a desire I respected. Plus, enough about me. In a moment, I'd ask about *his* private suffering, then demonstrate what unselfish listening looked like.

Was it selfish to wish that the person assigned the aisle seat beside me would miss their flight? I hoped the seven-foot basketball player in a hoodie carrying a puppy kept moving. Also, the cowboy-hat-wearing dude with briefcase. And please, no, I thought, not the man carrying a box of fried chicken who was slowing, looking, turning…into row 12. He fell into the seat ahead of me, opened the box and lifted a chicken part, which unleashed an aroma so strong and beautiful it sent me into my dead grandmother's kitchen.

To the monk, I said, "How do *you* contend with the psychic noise of childhood?"

"Sorry?" he said, pushing back an ear covering once more.

"How do you contend with noise?" I swirled my hand to indicate the plane's interior.

"What noise?"

"Ha. Right. But how do you get to that place where you can be so very much in the *now*, which is hard for me, especially with the weekend I had."

He pointed to his headphones and offered no invitation for me to explain my weekend.

"*My* trouble?" I said. "My imagination is always taking me beyond the moment. But I'm trying. I'll try again. Beginner's mind, right?"

He resumed reading, and I watched passengers move down the aisle, casting instant yes/no votes on a potential seatmate based on how much I imagined they'd evolved from their high school selves. *No,* I said to the person whose t-shirt featured the bulldog in a spiked collar who represented a major university's athletic program. The bulldog-shirt-wearer passed a bulldog-hat-wearer, said, "Sic 'em." The hat-wearer echoed him, a greeting of solidarity that made me jealous, oddly, though their tired voices made me imagine their team had suffered a soul-crushing defeat. "I'm sorry for your loss," I whispered. Then said, "Sic 'em," more loudly, to no one in particular. The monk looked up, confused.

The aisle cleared, attendants closed overhead bins, and I got excited that the aisle seat would go unclaimed. I considered moving over as a compassionate gesture to offer space, but it would make talking more difficult. Then a passenger stepped aboard whose eyes went instantly to the seat. They talked loudly on an invisible phone for everyone's benefit. Familiar voice. Familiar face. Familiar suit and tie. As the face and voice got closer, I saw, of course, that it was the raging lunatic who had earlier abused the gate-worker.

"Of course," I said.

The monk sighed heavily too, feeling the same disappointment, no doubt. He closed his book and crossed his arms as if to embrace the suffering caused by this hostile prick who dropped down with inconsiderate gusto, still talking loudly, promising the listener they'd be up fifteen percent by the close. He brushed against my shoulder and grunted because of the discomfort *I* was causing. The attendant closed and locked the cabin door, said please discontinue the use of mobile devices except as a flotation device.

The lunatic said, "An hour could ruin everything, but that's out of my control. I'm making peace. I'm concentrating on my breathing, playing it where it lies."

"Oh, please," I muttered. "Playing it where it lies."

The lunatic ended his call, then pointed across my lap to the monk's lap, said, "That's a good book. I'm quoted on page 88."

The book was called *The Radical Zen of Wall Street*. The cover featured a bull wearing a ring through its nose, atop which sat a Dalai Lama type figure, eyes closed, fully robed, palms on knees facing up. I felt betrayed. The raging lunatic reached inside his coat pocket to retrieve a business card he passed across my lap while brushing against my shoulder (emitting another sigh). The fake monk, seeing the name on the card, gushed like a kid meeting Spider-Man. He removed his headphones, said, "An honor," then bowed to the asshole. He dug into a bag at his feet to pull out his own card that he passed beneath the coffee I lifted to accommodate them. When the fake monk pulled his arm back, I lowered my coffee cup so it collided with his arm, then popped the lid with my thumbs and dumped my coffee onto the lap of He-Who-Is-Quoted-on-Page-88. Clearly, it appeared intentional. Because it was.

You would think the fool had been set on fire.

"Son of a motherfucking bastard," he shouted, and jumped into the aisle. He yelled for the flight attendant, pointed to his crotch, then at me, said, "This fool dumped hot coffee on my lap, which is aggravated assault, and I'd like him removed as a security risk." The flight attendant stared at me like *Would you care to deny or defend or explain any of this silly shit?*

I surrendered. I said, quite calmly, "I'd love to be removed."

The lunatic stepped back to let me by. He said, "You need to get some fucking help, psycho-freak—you're lucky I don't sue your fat ass back to the stone ages."

Which sounded excessive. My peaceful exit was a spectacle—the flight attendant reopening the cabin door, the light flooding in, me walking out to applause, the door closing behind me. I trudged up the empty tunnel, as heavy-footed and as slow as the last man on Earth. I made it as far as the gate I'd just left, empty now, sat near the window and watched my plane (and my checked bag!) back away.

My phone said 7% battery life remaining.

I knew I should let Maria know I'd been delayed, but I didn't want to explain the reasons. No need to call Mom, who might wonder whether I'd changed at all since that time I urinated on a teacher's desk. I didn't know if my credit card could handle another flight. Maybe I'd been declared a threat to national security and put on a no-fly list.

I reactivated social media. No notifications. But there was Blake, tagged in a group photo of reunion-goers posing in front of the pool with half-hearted smiles. I wasn't in the shot, of course. Which was fine. That seemed right. I scrolled through Blake's timeline to see the tributes, the pics of good times, the RIPs, the broken-heart emojis, most from people I didn't know. Then there were Blake's two little girls, laughing in a pumpkin patch, then his wife neck-deep in waters off Greece, then Blake smiling wide from behind a piano in New Orleans.

I walked. It helped to move, to stay in motion even while standing on the sliding sidewalks. I watched the news carried in every weary face and tired body, the walking wounded hauling their histories, lugging grief and regrets, navigating the limbo that came from taking one's head above the clouds then reintroducing it, only partially, to Earth. They exited planes, turned one way, reversed, collided, continued. People with canes, in wheelchairs, in beeping carts, people running for tight connections, toward loved ones who were dead or dying. Blake's face popped up in crowds of people who veered around me. I saw him in a bathroom, standing at a urinal. On a shoeshine stand. At the end of a bar, drinking a beer. I stopped and called his name. The stranger turned to me, and I walked away. I put my hand on the sliding handrail of a moving sidewalk and imagined all the germs I was collecting from so many millions of hands, then pulled my handkerchief from my back pocket and kept it on the sliding handrail for cleaning. Did the same with the next. And on escalators. My handkerchief turned black. How long would it take to wipe every handrail in the airport? Could I get a job cleaning the airport?

In another hour, my phone said 1%. I wasn't tempted to buy a new charger. I looked forward to my phone's death. I walked for hours, winding through every concourse. Entered a train at some random spot and exited at another and kept walking without looking at signs. I walked until my shoes wore blisters on my feet and kept walking. I walked until my legs grew numb and said they could walk no more, then I entered an empty gate and went to a row of chairs near the windows so I'd disturb fewer people. I made a couch of the seats and slept.

When I woke it was because Blake had grabbed my shoulder with a clawed hand and said, "Sounds good." It was dark now and the world made sense. I sat up, faced the windows and listened to a group seated behind me speaking a language I couldn't place. I couldn't decipher the meaning of a single word, but I understood the weariness from exhausted and exiled travelers. I could see all the way back to Maria, who would be worried now, so I sent her a message, telepathically, that I was on the way, that I was eager to show her how what I'd just this moment learned would save our lives. But I was in no hurry. I wanted to stay longer among these strangers and listen to the music in their language, so familiar and strange and suddenly so welcoming.

How Would You Like the Remains?

When Karl came home that Friday morning after working three straight nights at the fire station, he found Kim sitting at the kitchen table, where she announced that this was the day, finally, that they would adopt a cat from the Humane Society so she'd have *someone* to talk to. Karl cocked his head and scratched his ear. He opened the fridge, stared into the emptiness and whimpered. Hadn't they talked about this? His allergies. The odor and hassle of litter boxes, the vomit that ruined floors and carpets, the claws that ripped furniture and skin? Hadn't he made himself clear six months ago, just before they married and moved into their fixer-upper with the old floors he would soon be refinishing?

"What do you care?" she said. "You're never here." She paused to let the question rhyme with *divorce*. She stared with the unblinking eyes of a feline whose thoughts went from murder to cuddling, or cuddling to murder, Karl couldn't know.

At the Humane Society, he pointed to a playful Calico, and she pointed to a narcoleptic black kitten with *bad luck* stamped on its head, wild eyes that emitted horror. She said no one else would adopt it except at Halloween, when creeps did evil things with them.

"That's not—is that true?" Karl said.

"We'll call him Grendel," she said.

At home, Grendel prowled around with a monster-like strut and stomped up the stairs and across the floors. He hissed and flashed his fangs when Karl reached out to him, then cocked his paw, eager to decapitate. Karl's eyes had started itching at the Humane Society, and now they were burning, swelling shut. His nose felt clogged with cotton; his throat was closing. He sneezed three times, like shotgun blasts, and Grendel hissed, perturbed with the disturbance.

"Isn't he beautiful?" Kim said. "The great thing is we can leave him alone with food for a couple days if you ever got crazy and wanted to go somewhere."

"Let's go," Karl said, surprising himself, thinking he looked real good right about now, saying yes to cats and trips, saying yes, he'd heard Kim begging to go somewhere—anywhere—over the last half-year while he worked overtime or busied himself with home-repair projects or helped neighbors with theirs or helped his father across town, or helped a coworker get drunk at a faraway cabin while fishing. Secretly, he hoped she'd say no. *How sweet*, he hoped to hear, but she couldn't possibly leave Grendel on the same day she brought him home.

"I'm ready," she said.

Within one minute, she booked a room in an upstate resort she'd had her eye on, three hours away, which she promised they could afford because she'd just sold a new bathroom and kitchen (she created blueprints for contractors). When they walked into the high-ceilinged white lobby full of giant plants, Karl thought only of how they could afford no such a place. The big-smiling desk clerk who checked them in—a pencil-necked kid who bragged that he'd just earned a degree in Hospitality Management—informed them that his only ambition in life was to make people happy, and he smiled at Kim in a way that made Karl's stomach hurt.

His sleep schedule was off and the drive in a heavy rain had deepened his fatigue, so after dinner in the hotel's restaurant where he noted Kim's eighteen-dollar cocktail and his six-dollar beer and the outrageously priced tiny entrees, he said he must sleep, that she should play the slots, have a good time, that he'd be ready for fun the following morning.

It took Karl twenty years to learn that the fun she had that night came at the hands of the hospitality expert. He would learn that Kim and the kid had kept in touch as he advanced from desk clerk to manager, that she visited several times while Karl slept at the fire station, that she created blueprints for redesign projects that would improve the resort, that she admired the guy's ambition for wanting so badly to make people happy.

The next morning, Karl agreed to a "hike" around a mile-long loop with no destination in mind, then bragged about his ability to lie perfectly still beside the pool while Kim read her thousand-page novel. He did not dwell on the second night's expensive dinner. During the three-hour drive home, while Kim continued reading, he pondered the work ahead of him. When they pulled into the driveway, they heard Grendel howling like a demon-possessed coyote. Had he been howling all weekend?

"Poor guy," Kim said. "We have to get him another cat for company."

Karl sneezed, still inside his truck.

"Animals need their own kind," she said. "It's the humane thing to do."

"I'm going to work now," Karl answered, and did.

Three days later, he came home to wild and wicked sounds coming from inside the house. Kim sat on the couch, reading, seemingly unbothered by the needle-to-the-brain evil shrieks coming from behind the closed door of the guestroom. He pictured a pack of wolves, blood dripping from fangs, eyeballs stuck to claws. Objects flew off the walls and bookcases, shattering. He stared at Kim, waiting for her to look up from her book.

"That's Charlotte and Emily," she said. "They're working it out with Grendel."

"Working what out? You got *two*—"

"They're sisters. I couldn't *separate* them. They're establishing the hierarchy. It's what they do for a little while, then they'll be fine."

Named after the Brontes, she explained. She'd been a literature major in college and was always giving Karl books she hoped would give him a glimpse of beauty, slow him down, make him *imagine* different lives and what might be learned by watching people make mistakes. He never read them. What energy remained at the ends of days, drained from work? Just now, eyes burning, throat closing, he turned from the noise and went outside to hear something more pleasant, such as chainsaws, leaf blowers, lawnmowers, weed whackers. Which is when he discovered six feral cats sitting together in front of the garage like they belonged on stage. He went inside, brought Kim back out, pointed.

"Do you even have a heart?" she said. "Look how skinny they are. You have to get them spayed and neutered."

"*I* do? And who pays for that? And then what?"

"Do you want a *hundred* wild cats? That's what we'll have if you don't do it. Afterwards, they can hang out here because our shelter is a kill shelter and they'll die there. We'll feed them so they don't kill birds and ruin the ecosystem. It's the humane thing to do."

"No way," Karl said. "Nine cats is getting into crazy-cat-lady territory."

"Don't be sexist," she said.

The first five were easy. Canned food in traps, no problem. The last one was wise, but he was also starving, so when he got close, Karl grabbed him, squeezed, fought against the fierce wiggling (such a strong fucker), knowing he had one chance, and by the time he pushed him in and closed the door and stood, blood flowed from both arms and dripped off his fingertips.

"We'll call that one Edward," Kim said. "After Scissorhands. You should go to the ER after you drop him off. See if you need stitches."

Karl dropped the cat off at the vet, where they were eager for short-notice spaying and neutering chances, then drove himself to the ER, got six stitches in one arm, five in the other, plus an allergy-fighting nasal steroid and a pack of antihistamines, then went back for Edward, brought him home and turned him loose among the herd that soon came to own the place. They lay on the front stoop and around the yard and on the back patio like a fat and happy family, pooping and pissing in flowerbeds they made their own.

The next morning, Kim opened the door where Grendel, Charlotte, and Emily had worked it out. Grendel emerged last, tail between his legs.

"See?" Kim said. "All's well."

Grendel went straight for Karl, who lay comfortably on the couch, full of decongestants, jumped on his chest and started purring, which Karl found strange and relaxing. Grendel started following him around the house. He perched on Karl's shoulders while he sat on the toilet. Karl put him on a leash and they went for walks. They sat beneath the birch tree out back and watched birds. The other cats shunned them. Karl took him on rides around town, cracked the passenger-side window so he could stick his nose out and gulp the air. When Karl came home after working three consecutive nights, Kim reported that Grendel howled with happiness as soon as he heard Karl's truck. In bed, Grendel lay on Karl's chest and stared into his eyes, purring so loudly his heart vibrated against Karl's chest. Their breathing synced up. Karl looked into Grendel's eyes and saw a deep mirror of soulful mysteries neither of them could articulate.

The years passed while they worked and slept, procreated, raised two children, remodeled rooms, replaced appliances, planted vegetables and flowers, finished the basement, painted and repainted, helped neighbors, bought cars, buried parents, sent one kid to college, one to rehab. Karl entered burning buildings, resuscitated dead people, held hands with the dying, said he'd rather not talk about work when he wasn't working, and didn't. He missed parent-teacher conferences, ball games, recitals, hospital trips for minor injuries, driver's license tests, car wrecks, school plays, proms, etc. They said they understood. On nights at home, they ate ice cream and watched their shows, cats in laps, outside cats lounging too, fat and happy.

Over the years, the cat population dwindled. Virginia got attacked by a loose dog, a horrible scene Karl hated that the children witnessed, then Woolf, Edith, and Wharton disappeared after seven, nine, and ten years, long lives for outdoor cats, Kim said, then Edward got run over, then Emily suffered an aneurysm that paralyzed her back legs, and by the time they scooped her up and rushed her to the vet, her heart was nearing paralysis too, then Charlotte stopped eating and died of grief, apparently, then Karl backed over Sylvia in the driveway. He called in sick that day. Stomach pains put him on the couch, where Grendel, their first and last, lay on his chest, purring, staring into his eyes. The old man was almost twenty now, just like that, and except for a few white hairs hanging from his chin, weight loss, slower steps, lethargy, incontinence, and leakage issues, he was perfectly fine.

One early morning, a week after their daughter left for college, and with their son in rehab, Kim approached Karl, who was lying on the couch with Grendel on his chest again, facing three days off he wanted to spend doing *nothing*.

"You should do the humane thing," Kim said. "End his suffering."

He petted Grendel's sleeping head. He didn't purr. Didn't move. "We're fine," he said.

"Those daily shots you give him? Those are more for you than him, you know."

"You should see him when we step into the vet's office. You've never heard anything so alive. We're going again this afternoon to get our anal glands expressed."

"Listen," she said. Like he'd never understood the word. And it was then, while standing, facing the door, that she announced she was leaving for the same resort they'd visited twenty years ago—the last time they went anywhere, she added—to meet with the manager about a redesign project, and she couldn't say when she'd be back.

And Karl said, "Oh. Okay."

She gave Karl a look he'd remember later that night—a *goodbye and good luck* kind of look he thought was aimed more at Grendel than him.

At three o'clock, he loaded Grendel (without his usual protest) into his carrier and drove him to the vet, talking to him, reassuring him that he'd feel better soon. When they stepped into the vet's office, Grendel did not deliver his customary eardrum-splitting, Africa-infused, soul-shrieking, dead-awakening howl. He carried him to the waiting area and sat beside a big man in a camo tank top, the nearest shoulder covered in a tiger-face tattoo. The man bent toward the carrier in his lap, nose to the gate, said, "Dat's a pretty putty tat." Then sniffed. Across from Karl sat an old man in a wheelchair, legs gone at the knees, a wrinkled and worried face, like he'd been crying or would soon. His hat said *Vietnam Vet*, and for a minute Karl confused "vet" for veterinarian and grew curious about Eastern animal medicine. Then it occurred to him, with great clarity, that he might soon die of dementia, worry-free.

Camo-guy sniffed again.

"Tough day, huh?" Karl said.

The man tried to speak, stopped, sniffed, wiped his nose, said, "Yup."

The vet said, "They break your goddamned heart every motherfucking time. My kitty's in surgery after he swallowed a heart pill I dropped last night. Last summer, he lost an eye after he got snake bit. That surgery cost me $1,000. I told my wife then, I said, I can't take another scare like that one."

Camo-guy said, "This is my daughter's cat. She's off at college, and I'm going to have to call her in a few minutes and tell her we had to put Fluffy down and she'll end up trying to comfort me, which don't seem right."

"Every goddamned time," the vet said.

"We're just getting our anal glands expressed," Karl said.

"My one-eyed cat has diabetes and no teeth," the vet said. "He got allergic to the enamel on his teeth, strangest damn thing. I give him a shot of insulin every afternoon at five o'clock, right before his dinner. Jumps on my lap and takes his medicine just like that. Hell of a lot braver than I am, tell you the awful goddamn truth about it."

They paused to appreciate the awful truth.

"It was easier when my father died," Camo-guy said. "He didn't understand cats' ways. Thought they were dirty. But you don't see a dog grooming itself the way a cat grooms itself."

"Or each other," Karl said, thinking of the tongue baths Emily and Charlotte and the outside cats had offered each other, though never Grendel.

"I won't sleep tonight if he don't make it," the vet said. "He curls up on my neck and we go to sleep like that." He put his hand on his neck to demonstrate. "Then he touches my nose at 5 a.m., says *breakfast time*. Gentlest little touch you ever saw."

Camo-guy said, "This one crawls on my shoulder and suckles my ear lobe."

"I've never had one to suckle an earlobe," the vet said.

"There's nothing like a cat purr," Karl said. "This one's got a diesel engine."

Camo-guy said, "I read somewhere that if you've got a body ache, you should put a purring cat on it. Even a headache."

"Heartache too," the vet said. "My wife died last December, and my cat's the only thing got me through."

"Animals are better than us," Camo-guy said. "My wife got chemo last year, and what kept her going back was looking forward to seeing that therapy dog there."

"Hope," the vet said.

"That's right," Camo-guy said.

"That's the dog's name," the vet said. "Hope. My wife got chemo there too. That was the prettiest blue-eyed dog you've ever seen."

"My wife died last August a year ago," Camo-guy said. "Then my daughter went to college and left me home with her cat, who helped me through, like you say."

"My wife was ready," the vet said. "Truth is, I helped her along a little bit, tried to make it peaceful, which was the right thing to do, whether it's legal or not. This cat was hers first, and I'm not sure how I'm going to make it without either one of them, be honest with you."

"I can't work today," Camo-guy said. "Called in sick. At least it's summer and the ground's not frozen. I know a guy whose cat died last winter, so he kept him on the porch for a couple months until the ground thawed out enough to bury him. Laid him in a chair and said hello every time he went in or out."

Karl and the vet nodded as if they knew the guy.

"It's a lonely feeling when you come home and nobody's there," the vet said.

"We're just getting our anal glands expressed," Karl said again, and the men nodded.

In a few minutes, a sad-eyed lady came out and called for the vet, who rolled away.

"Best of luck to you," Camo-guy told him, and he said, "Y'all too."

A different lady came out a minute later and called for Fluffy. Camo-guy stood, lifted the carrier to eye level, said, "Here we go, sweet girl."

"Good luck," Karl said, and Camo-guy said, "You too."

The first lady came back, called for Grendel, and led Karl into room #4, the special calming room they always made available for him because of his infamously loud protests, but he was strangely silent now. Grendel's vet for the past twenty years, Dr. Metzendorf, had died just three months ago, an apparent suicide, though no one came right out and said so, maybe it was bad for business, but Kim knew the sister of his neighbor's contractor, who said he'd given himself a lethal dose of the same stuff he'd had to give his horse, and they found him with his head lying on his horse's neck, which Kim said was a courageous way to go if you'd already thought long and hard about it. He was seventy-five, had retired, then returned, then did what he did.

The new vet, Dr. Megan, was young, just getting a taste of the life she'd signed up for. She looked like she'd already had a bad morning and knew she was headed for worse. She gave Karl a tired smile, peeked at Grendel, looked over his records.

"She's not doing so well, huh?" she said.

"*He*," Karl said.

She put her hands on his backside and he didn't react, which was strange. She put her stethoscope on his chest. She looked him over and he did not resist.

"His kidneys are non-functional," she said. "They're really good at hiding their pain, but I'm afraid it's maybe time to think about his quality of life and whether you'd like to ease his suffering for the little bit of time he has left."

Karl bent and looked at him. His eyes were glassy, distant.

"I'll step out for a minute," she said. "Let you think about it. Have a moment. I know it's hard. When I come back, you can tell me what you'd like to do."

Karl looked at Grendel, lying on his side, head down, eyes nearly closed.

He said, "Say something." Karl lifted his weightless front paw. "Is this what you want, buddy?" Karl said. Grendel didn't answer.

Dr. Megan came back in, handed Karl a box of Kleenex, said she was so very sorry, etc., she'd had a good life, etc. What else can you say? Then her assistant stepped in with a credit card machine. She looked tired and depressed too, like she'd already been through some deaths today and had more scheduled.

"How would you like the remains?" she said.

Karl didn't understand, which must've been obvious.

"Cremation, or would you like to take her home, or—"

"*Him*. I'll take him home."

Dr. Megan held a needle and a bottle.

"This will be quick," she said.

Karl held Grendel's paw. He bent toward his ear and whispered that he loved him.

He carried him out in a box through the back door the assistant held open.

"I'm sorry," she said. "She was a beautiful cat."

"*He*," Karl said. "Thank you."

He didn't want to go home. It was a bright and hot afternoon toward the end of summer. He carried Grendel down the gravel path that wound around a rock garden between some hedges toward a shaded bench that faced a pond. A plaque bolted to the bench had Jacob Metzendorf's name on it, a cat paw beside it. He sat with Grendel on his lap, in his box, and stared at the water. Above the pond, a daytime bat made figure-eights. The ducks on the far side made a trip across the pond, then started back. The sun splintered light across the water filtered through a thick stand of trees. A single cloud crawled across the sky. Karl thought of Kim, how she was right, of course. Wasn't she always right? He should've ended Grendel's suffering sooner. He thought of his son and daughter and wanted to tell them how very much in tune he was right this second with the fragile nature of their brief lives. He wanted to apologize for the important events he'd missed and promise to be there for the next. He wanted to call Kim and offer to take her somewhere she'd always wanted to go while they were still young enough to move well. Europe? Paris? Sure, Paris.

She answered on the fourth ring.

"I put Grendel down," he said.

"Thank God. He suffered too long, poor guy."

She didn't sound too sympathetic. She sounded distracted, like she had more important things on her mind. He heard her shuffling papers. Blueprints?

"I have to tell you something," she said.

Karl watched the daytime bat swoop over the water, and he waited.

"I'm not coming home."

"What?"

She explained that Stefan had hired her to help run the place. She talked of how they'd been writing each other for twenty years, since that first night ("a spontaneous indiscretion") they discovered such compatibility, that the affair had been going on that long too, which she wasn't proud about, God knows, but couldn't Karl see how unhappy she'd been, and couldn't he be happy for her now that she had a purpose to her life, how she and Stefan were planning clubhouse renovations, new menus, a dining room redesign, and new recreational opportunities such as equestrian trail-riding? Soon, they'd be hosting major fundraising events for politicians. She apologized, again, for telling him so much so suddenly over the phone, but it was time to do the humane thing and end it quickly, which would hurt for a little while, she knew, but she imagined he'd lose himself in work, as he always had, and that he'd soon be okay.

Karl couldn't summon words. Was he having a stroke?

"I've been telling you this would happen," she said.

"You never—"

"I told you in many ways. I'm not going to hash it out now. It's just—lives are meant to be redesigned on occasion. Would you like to meet him?"

"What? No. I already—"

"If you'd like to visit for a weekend, I can get you a reduced rate."

He couldn't locate a single word. She said they could talk later if he wanted, then said she had to go, then said goodbye. He clutched Grendel's box. The ducks climbed out of the water on the far side of the pond. The daytime bat swooped in clumsy semi-circles, then vanished. Karl didn't know what day it was. He got out his phone and googled the resort and saw a photo of Stefan (decidedly older now, but still smiling) standing against a golden sunset, holding one dog, a Shih Tzu or some-shit, while a bear-looking Mastiff, sat beside him, facing the camera.

What gets into people? What reaction can you muster when you think you're cruising along just fine and one day you're told you should've seen the collision coming? What could he have done? Listened better to what she wasn't saying? He remembered then the last novel she'd given him, just a year ago, which he didn't read, though he did watch the movie one slow night at the station, and the guys watched it with him, a movie about a butler and a housemaid who were deeply in love but too uptight and cowardly to say so, then suddenly they're old, staring into their dark cups of tea, regretting the lives they'd wasted and the few hours that remained of their days. He couldn't remember the title. He told her he'd liked it, how all the guys liked it too, even though nothing much ever happened and then suddenly the characters were old and almost dead, which they figured was the point. Then he and the guys got back to work, craving rest.

He stayed on the bench for another hour, staring at the water, the years beneath it. When he smelled his skin burning from the high sun, he lifted Grendel and carried him to his truck, then home, then to his backyard where he dug a hole beneath the birch tree and sat for a long while beside it, drinking whiskey until the whiskey was gone. He waved at his neighbor—the weird guy named Marty that Karl had tried to befriend, who now accelerated his pace, just as he did every time Karl waved. He hoped he might stop this time, maybe listen for a minute to the story of Karl's day, but he sped up instead, again, until he vanished into his house.

Then it was dark and Karl was drunk, sitting on the floor of his bedroom facing his empty bed, handgun in his lap. He called his daughter so she could say *Hey Daddy* and remind him who he was. No answer. Then he called his son, who was in rehab and did not answer. He texted Kim. He texted all sorts of things he wouldn't have texted had he been himself, and sober. Then a cop came in, shouting something about a wellness check. Then Karl decided to shoot his bed, his walls, his ceiling. The cop reported shots fired, which brought the BearCat and SWAT team and the entire PD., who barricaded two city blocks. A trained mediator called and kept him on the phone, told long stories of all the pets he'd loved and lost and three divorces he'd survived and four kids who'd moved across the country and rarely spoke to him. He talked of how all the guys Karl worked with to save lives were rooting for him to come out safely so they could harass him and say, *what the fuck's wrong with you, increasing our workload?* And exhausted, weeping, Karl surrendered. First to jail, then to a faraway facility, then to a release without a job to return to, though many good folks said *good luck.*

But just before that, just before Kim told him what he later realized took her some courage to say, he wanted to rush toward her and toward their children as if they were on fire. He wanted to say *here I am*. That was the feeling he wanted to cling to while he worked days at a hardware store and nights as a bartender. He moved into an elderly couple's basement who charged him no rent because he repaired their steps, painted the trim, and refinished the floors.

The following summer, his children answered his calls more often. They lived with their mother, worked at the resort, and liked it. They suggested he visit. *Sure*, he said. *Maybe so.* He thought about it as Thanksgiving approached, but his boss depended on him to open the hardware store early every morning. He thought about it again as winter moved in and Christmas neared. He imagined their surprised faces the moment he entered the lobby and found them all sitting together beside the fire. He pictured them watching him limp forward, how he'd have to explain it was just a couple of bad knees and a stiff back, nothing to worry about. Soon, he thought. Very soon. He liked to imagine that moment he could take his damaged heart to them, drop it at their feet and present it as a gift.

Please Pass the Flotsam

I didn't like to think before coffee, but Dr. Death was coming for dinner, so my first thought of the morning had to do with the dread of the evening and my fear that I would behave quite badly. If I behaved badly enough, Maria promised a rapid divorce with zero custody. So I tried not to think about it. I walked into the kitchen and moved past her, seated at the table, eight months pregnant, phone in hand, and when I got to where my cup was supposed to be—the cup I rinsed every night to use every morning so I could save dishwasher space and reduce energy consumption—it wasn't there, and she said, "Oh my God, they've had a shipwreck."

"Where's my cup?" I said.

"Holy shit," she said. "They almost died."

She had a tendency toward ambiguous pronoun usage when reporting news from her phone. It was irritating. I looked in the dishwasher.

"They're okay," she said. "But damn—*a shipwreck!*"

Before we married, ten years ago, I'd asked that our morning protocol forbid serious talk BC (Before Coffee). I meant to honor my side of the agreement.

"I left it on the counter last night," I said.

"What're you talking about?" she said.

"What're *you* talking about?"

"Teri, Luke, and Lou," Maria said, like I'd missed that part. "They've been in a fucking shipwreck in the middle of Lake Michigan."

"Are they okay?"

"I just said they were okay."

Had she? Our friends Luke and Teri and their seven-year-old, Lou, were on the way to see us in Wisconsin, via Michigan, from Hawaii, where they'd moved three years ago. For jobs! Were we jealous? Of course. We threw them a going away party, and tonight we were hosting a welcome back party of sorts, though only one of their other friends was coming, Finn, aka Dr. Death, a depressed ex-science professor whose life's-purpose was to make sure we kept our calendars updated for our upcoming extinction. He said we'd passed the proverbial tipping point, that the only hope was radical population control via mandatory vasectomies. At the going-away party, I'd caught him in the kitchen flirting with Maria, both of them drunk, heard him say something stupid like the species should go out with a bang. Which was when I approached and pushed his shoulder (a tad too forcefully) and invited him to go fuck himself. Maria called me a jealous child, the party dissipated, and I spent the night on the couch and the next three days apologizing, groveling. She said, "Just because he's brilliant and sexy doesn't mean I'd do anything; stop being so insecure. It's gross." Brilliant? I guess *he'd* agree. He talked a lot about himself, how he'd grown up in Germany, attended Berkeley for his PhD, joined an eco-terrorist group in Oregon, lived off-grid in his thirties, built a house in New Mexico from old tires and bottles (an Earthship!), then took a teaching job in Wisconsin and developed a cult following among students and colleagues. I didn't like him. But Luke liked him, and I liked Luke, so I gritted my teeth and told Luke he could invite him. Luke and Teri were solid and fair-minded Midwesterners, people I'd want on my jury should I murder Dr. Death.

"Your coffee cup's outside where you left it," Maria said.

I pulled out a new cup, filled it, added almond milk. Six months ago, Maria announced we were going from vegetarians to vegans. Not so hard, really.

"Their boat capsized," Maria said. "Luke's father's boat. Teri's texting me on her mother's phone. They're really shaken up."

"Is a capsize the same as a shipwreck?" I said.

"You just put the almond milk in the cupboard. I've asked you to stop buying it because—as Finn told us last time—it takes one gallon of water to produce a single almond and the water situation in California is fucked, except for the almond owners, as we've discussed."

Had we? Last week, she found a bag of frozen spinach in the closet. Yesterday, when I locked myself out of the house again, I said I should get tested for early onset whatever-you-call-it, ha-ha. I blamed my absent-mindedness on her pregnancy, which didn't go over well. It was partly true; I stayed distracted with worry. I was nearly forty, an unskilled and unemployed non-laborer, anxious over the world my child would inhabit if I didn't kill her first by leaving her in a locked car. We squeaked by on Maria's teaching job, and I had helped briefly by teaching fourth grade, first as a substitute, then as full-time temporary, but I couldn't keep track of names, and one day when I corrected a kid's grammar, he mocked my southern accent, which led me to calling him a little shit, which led the principal to expel me. So I returned to being a househusband and tried to make Maria happy. Daily trips to Trader Joe's for vegan food and eco-friendly cleaning products. Between shopping, cooking, and cleaning, I watched YouTube videos for how to install low-flush toilets (in progress) and ways to maximize energy efficiency, which led to despair because I had no know-how, which led to hours on the internet and another hour erasing my history. Lately, I spent my afternoons staring into the sinkhole in front of our house. City crews were working on it, running big machines that backed up and beeped, backed up and beeped—*all day*—stretching hoses down the street they'd plowed up. Our town was in the midst of a sinkhole epidemic. I couldn't wait to hear Finn's opinion on the topic.

"Are you going to behave tonight?" Maria said.

I pointed to my full coffee cup and didn't answer.

Dr. Death was anti-air conditioning, and since *his* comfort was key, we'd be eating outside, where we'd enjoy another record-setting day over one hundred degrees. He'd developed an actual air conditioning allergy (allegedly), claimed we should all be conditioning ourselves toward hotter times, that we shouldn't fool ourselves into feeling comfortable while the planet burned. Meanwhile, the Wisconsin natives were going nuts. A middle-aged man beat an elderly man to death after arguing over a parking space at a home improvement store. A walker on a bike trail clotheslined a biker. Road-raging lunatics fired pistols. Everywhere, people seethed with anger, waiting for the smallest excuse to yell profanities and raise middle fingers.

"Of course I'll behave," I said. "No problem." And I hoped it was true. I'd agreed to take care of everything if Maria agreed to rest. I'd clean the backyard, arrange seating, fill coolers with ice, beer, water, set up fans, mosquito-fighting accessories, pick up food we'd pre-ordered from the Co-op at great expense, be a pleasant host, make sure Dr. Death stayed happy.

Maria got the long-handled duster from the cupboard, then stepped on an unstable chair to knock down spiderwebs.

"That's not safe," I said, and went outside.

When I went for the mower, I discovered my gas can had been stolen. These were the end times all right. People were desperate. When I reported this news to Maria, she came to the garage and pointed to the can sitting on top of the upright piano I'd salvaged last month.

"Someone *moved* it," I said, hoping she'd laugh, but she'd already walked away.

I drove to the gas station to fill the can, forgot the beer and ice, returned, then mowed, then went out again for tiki torches, scented candles, an extra fan and extension cord, and when I next saw Maria, I was in a chair beneath our dying elm tree, near the bottom of my third gluten-free beer, a recipe that helped me discover I was not, in fact, allergic to alcohol and could therefore *Drink Wisconsibly*, as the t-shirts say.

She said, "Did you plan to shower and pick up the food *before* our guests arrived?"

"Of course," I said, like I hadn't lost track of time.

Maria told me three times to make sure the Mediterranean bean dish entrée was *not* topped with cheese. It was. The youngster I dealt with fetched his manager, who came with a copy of the order and showed me the empty space beneath the "special requests" box, which meant it was my fault. I imagined Maria's face and couldn't bear the disappointment, then I imagined Finn accusing me of sustaining the dairy industry (in Wisconsin!) which was killing us because of the land required to grow cow food versus vegetables, plus runoff from poop and pee, plus cow farts. They prepared a new dish.

When I got home, Luke, Teri, and Lou had just pulled into our driveway and Maria was greeting them, sporting a nice (new?) sundress. For Finn? I wasn't a jealous guy, normally, but I couldn't forget the way he'd flirted with her. *Stay cool*, I told myself. Our friends were here, and I was glad. We welcomed them as if they'd returned from war.

"We had a shipwreck," said Lou. He was seven now, a smart kid.

"I know," I said. "Do you need a drink?"

"What's going on here?" Teri said, pointing to our sinkhole, the stretched out hoses, the yellow backhoe parked in our street.

"More of a boating accident," Luke said, and laughed that hair-trigger laugh of his.

"We're installing a swimming pool," Maria said.

"I'll take a drink," Lou said. "Water with no ice, please."

We led them out back to chairs in front of the two fans I'd arranged to create enough breeze to discourage mosquitoes and break the heat. It was nearly 7 p.m. by then, temps moving from unbearable to uncomfortable. The fans surrounded scented candles and tiki torches surrounded the fans. They exhaled, happy to be free of cars and boats, roads and water.

Maria slapped her neck.

"Your blood type is attractive," said Lou.

"Thank you, Lou," Maria said, and we laughed.

It was easy to laugh with them. We'd missed doing so for the past three years. Maria and Teri met when they found themselves volunteering with the urban gardening task force, the homeless task force, the hunger task force, a save-the-marsh task force, etc. They had us over, we had them over, found it comforting to be in their calming presence, which I hoped was mutual, though I suspected we clung to them more than they needed us, and when Lou was born, they clung to him, as you expect, just as we would soon cling to whatever came out of Maria. Other universities recruited Luke; he got offers his department couldn't match. He narrowed his choices to a big university in Alabama (more money, light teaching load, top-shelf labs) and a college in Hawaii (less money, heavy teaching load, poorer labs). They came for drinks and dinner, asked our opinions.

"Neither," Maria had said. "You can't leave us stranded here."

"Did I hear you say," I said, "more money to teach fewer classes? That's a no-brainer."

They took less money and more work to live in Hawaii. A year later, when we saw the footage of lava explosions flooding through streets and flattening homes, we kept calling and texting to see if they were okay, but we never heard from them. Teri was out helping people and Luke was conducting drone-based research on the lava. When the lava-rivers cooled enough for Teri to finally write, she said, "We're fine. Luke says we're lucky to be here in the middle of all this, but it's traumatic, explosions every thirty seconds. I'm getting used to the dinosaur-sized roaches who sleep with us. More later." They'd survived the lava, got nicked by a typhoon, and now they'd survived near-drownings, and seemed, still, to be the ones worth clinging to.

I wanted to hear about Hawaii, ask about their guest bedroom, fish for an invitation to visit, but before I could say much at all, Dr. Death came strolling around back wearing his bike helmet and backpack, wine bottle in hand, a t-shirt that featured an image of an hourglass with a circle around it. Luke and Teri raced to him for hugs. He handed me the wine while staring at Maria. He put one hand on her bare shoulder and one hand on her bloated stomach.

"How did this happen?" he said. "You decide to bring a child into this dying world?"

"She's going to *save* the world," Maria said, and everyone laughed, even little Lou.

"We had a shipwreck!" Lou told him.

He sat next to Maria, of course, his left knee nearly touching her right. He kept his biking helmet on, unfastened. When I asked politely if he'd like beer, wine, liquor, or water, he said, "Yes!" And everyone laughed. A real comedian.

"More of a boating accident," Luke said, and giggled.

When I handed him a beer, he didn't thank me. He lofted it into the air.

"A toast!" he shouted.

Of course. I wished I'd beaten him to it.

"To death," Finn said.

"Beautiful," I said, and Maria shushed me.

"Our proximity to extinction," he continued, "is a gift from deep time that gives us a glimpse of the sublime, which invites us also to embrace the unknowable scheme of the universe." He paused, on the verge of tears. "Which is to say, we feel profound awe that you are *here*, to make us also feel so very much alive."

"Yes," Maria said, nearly singing. She clinked her wine glass against Finn's beer and they looked into each other's eyes. I clinked my beer against Lou's water.

"It *was* frightening," Luke said. He described how his father took them for a ride in his boat equipped with two motors, a small one for fishing and a big one to get through Lake Michigan's shipping channels.

"I had my doubts right away," he said. "I saw how the weight was distributed—the big motor weighed down the back of the boat, plus a big gas tank sitting in the rear, and he's a big guy. Maybe 250 pounds. I told him I didn't like it, but—"

"Dads are dumb," Maria said.

"I was dumb too," Luke said. "I should've been firmer. All that weight's in the back of the boat, and we're speeding out through the channel and hit a big wave at a bad angle and the front end flew up and sent us flying."

"The boat was *standing*!" Lou said, holding his palm up to demonstrate.

"And we're all in the water," Teri said, "and Luke's dad is yelling, *stay calm—stay close to the boat*, and I'm like no way dude because the boat looks like it's about to fall on top of us, so we swam away and watched the boat go down. It took thirty minutes. Then we're just hanging out, floating there by ourselves in the middle of Lake Michigan, clinging to flotsam. I've always wanted to use that word, *flotsam*."

"You were wearing PFDs, of course," Maria said.

"All but my dumb dad," Luke said.

"He shared my piece of flotsam," Teri said.

"Was the water cold?" Maria asked.

"What's flotsam?" Lou asked. He sat on the edge of his chair, eager to participate, fully on track to becoming a mad scientist or a tortured mathematician.

"More like forty-five minutes," Luke said.

"What's the difference between flotsam and jetsam?" I asked.

"It was *freezing*," Teri said.

"Remember the end of *Titanic*?" I said. "Was Leo clinging to flotsam or jetsam?"

"What *is* the difference?" Maria said.

No one reached for their phones. It was impressive.

"Flotsam," Finn said, "typically represents debris from wreckage that remains afloat. Jetsam is what might be discarded to prevent or delay sinking. Flotsam *and* jetsam are produced and owned by humans. These chairs. Candles. Fans. Extension cords. Tiki torches. Tables. Lawnmowers. Gasoline. That garage, the cars inside it, that house and everything it holds. Shingles. Everything you own, which now owns you as one ensnared in a capitalist trap."

I reached for my phone. I said, "There's a rock band called Flotsam and Jetsam."

"A giant freight ship almost saved us," Lou said.

"It started to turn around," Teri said. "Which was impressive. Something that big, it was going to take a while. A radical act of kindness."

"What were they hauling?" I asked.

"Jetsam," Finn said.

"But then this fisherman came along," Luke said. "He helped us climb into his boat and called the Coast Guard or rescue people or whoever."

"The water tasted like oil?" Finn said. "Shipping companies spend billions on devices to reroute pollution from the air to the water to hide it better. Open-loop scrubbers they are called."

Finn's voice made me want to drink. I got a new beer from the cooler, crumpled my empty can and considered hurling it at his head.

"The rescue people kept getting mad at the fisherman," Luke said.

"There are twenty-two *known* carcinogens floating in most water supplies," Finn said. "Arsenic. Radionuclides such as uranium and radium."

"For not saying 'over,' or 'copy,' or 'roger,' and the fisherman was like, 'Look, I've got these people in my boat, what should I do with them?' And they wouldn't answer, and the fisherman would be, like, 'Hello? Are you there?' And they'd get mad again because he hadn't said 'over.' I felt bad for the guy."

"The only ships should be Earthships," Finn said.

"Anyway," I said, trying to reroute the Earthship lecture Finn was queuing up. "Flotsam is what you were clinging to while waiting to be rescued."

"What's an Earthship?" said Lou, the little shit.

"Didn't you build your own Earthship, Finn?" said Maria.

And he was off, lecturing at great length about the house he'd built from bottles and tires and assorted garbage, how each drop of precious New Mexico rainwater got used three times, how he grew his garden in his living room, how he lived in a suburb of Earthships where neighbors pooled their resources and survived with zero electricity, needing nothing.

"But listen," I said to Luke. "While you were clinging to flotsam in the freezing water, did you tell your dad *I told you so?*"

Luke laughed, as if I'd meant to be funny. "No," he said. "That would've been counterproductive. I tried to keep things positive."

"He's always trying to keep things positive," Teri said, like this habit was testing their marriage. "Even after the boat went down, he was like, 'Would someone please pass some flotsam? Who's got some flotsam?'"

"Our best teacher arrives in the form of death," Finn said.

Maria swatted a mosquito. Finn pulled a small bottle from his pocket and passed it to her. "Vanilla extract," he said. "It will work for ten minutes. Soon, winter will be here, thank God."

"I miss Wisconsin winters," Teri said. "How it kills the creepy crawlies."

"Except ticks," Finn said. "Ticks burrow underground and return with greater immunity."

"Our neighbor has had Lyme disease three times," Maria said.

"My brother got a tick bite that gave him a meat allergy," Teri said. "Every time he ate meat he vomited."

"Excellent," Finn said. "We must breed that species of tick and drop them into meat-eaters' yards. Then take them into heavy beef-eating countries like Argentina."

"An opossum eats 10,000 ticks per week," Lou said. "Like M&M's."

"Do opossums eat termites?" I said.

"When we were in Albania," Teri said, "the termites were so bad in this place we stayed that we could hear them in the next room eating the wood. It kept us from sleeping. Then one night we heard a crash, and we went to look and saw the dining room table had collapsed. They'd eaten the legs right out from under it."

Finn laughed and clapped. "In an Earthship, there are no termites," he said.

Luke said, "After we boarded a plane from Albania to New Zealand, a flight attendant came down the aisle with a spray bottle she held over everyone's heads and sprayed us, without warning, without telling us what it was or why, which freaked us out. We covered our faces. We thought we were being gassed. And then *afterward*, like a genius, she got on the microphone and explained that she had just sprayed the plane to kill whatever we might be carrying on our clothes or shoes that could be invasive."

Maria swatted a mosquito. She said, "Please pass the vanilla extract." She touched Finn's forearm, I noticed, then offered her palm, into which he placed his vanilla extract.

"Where are the bats when you need them?" Teri asked.

"The northern long-ear is endangered," Finn said. "Also, wind energy kills too many bats and birds. Also, bats only reproduce about one pup per year."

"Reproduce only," I muttered, correcting his misplaced modifier.

"Over 2,000 animal species vanish each day," Finn said. "State birds are evacuating their states. The loons of Minnesota. Purple finches of New Hampshire. Brown thrashers of Georgia."

"It's so hot in Qatar, they're air conditioning the outdoors," Teri said.

"Do bats eat ticks?" I said.

"The ruffed grouse of Pennsylvania," Finn continued. "The goldfinch of New Jersey."

"We had a bat in our bedroom last week," Maria said.

"There are three billion fewer birds than fifty years ago," Finn said.

"He killed it," Maria said, pointing at me.

"I tried to shoo it out with a box lid," I said. "I didn't *want* to kill it. Last week, I freed a bat from a mousetrap."

Maria gave me a horrified look. Everyone else looked too, awaiting an explanation.

"I found it like that," I said, then explained how its wing had gotten caught in the trap I'd placed on a basement ledge, how it had fallen to the ground, trap and all, so I scooped it up with a dustpan and carried it outside, opened the spring with a screwdriver, then watched it scuttle away. Maybe a stronger man could have killed it so it wouldn't die a more painful death from starvation, but I couldn't do it. I gave it a sporting chance.

"I released it," I said.

Everyone looked at me like suddenly *I* was a bigger party pooper than Finn.

"You can get traps that won't hurt mice," Luke said. "Then take them out at dusk and toss them in a thick patch of grass for owls to feed on."

Another pause. Finn looked into the darkening sky, suddenly somber, as if he were about to pray, or say something profound. Maria looked at the same spot as if she were seeing what he was seeing. I finished another beer.

"I would like to see one more eclipse," Finn said. Then he talked of how wonderful it had been the previous August when he'd met Teri, Luke, and Lou in Nebraska so they could experience two minutes and forty-two seconds of totality. So beautiful, he said. Which made me jealous. Why hadn't we been invited?

"It was like a sunset turned inside out," Finn said.

"Major chills," Teri said.

"Like we ingested dawn," Finn said.

"This old guy in a long beard and black robe kept running around yelling the Messiah's here, the Messiah's here," Luke said.

"Did you film it?" Maria said.

"No," Teri said. "But everyone else did. Later, we saw a clip with our faces on it. The filmmaker panned around to capture the faces looking at the eclipse, and there we were. We saw our faces like we'd never seen them before. It was weird."

"I doubt I'll be alive to see the next one," Finn said.

"Jesus H. *Christ*," I blurted. I had heard enough. "What a fucking buzzkill," I said. "You make me feel like pouring gasoline on myself and lighting a match. Remind me in a few months to invite you over so you can tell our child that he shouldn't bother leaving the crib."

"*She*," Maria said, and giggled, trying to cut the tension.

Teri said, "Finn, would you be comfortable sharing your news?

"I have pancreatic cancer," he said. "Stage 4.5 or something." He looked at me then and laughed a lips-closed kind of laugh. "I might miss the next eclipse," he said. "But also the apocalypse. Win some, lose some. But please, no pity. Death and I are friends."

His face was pale, I noticed then. Dark rings around his eyes. Thinner than I remembered. Pointy cheek bones. A skeleton with acne scars. Maria studied his face more closely now too, in a way that suggested (or so it seemed) that he was more attractive now. Which I almost understood. Of course, I felt like shit. Maria looked at me like I should feel worse.

I stood. I said, "I'm sorry, Finn. That was—I'm sorry."

"No pity," he said. "Let us act toward each other as if all of us are dying soon. Let us surrender to the wonder that is the incomprehensible mystery of deep time."

No one said anything. We wanted to honor the pause.

"A toast," I said. I paused to think of words. "To friends," I said. "Especially Lou, who has time to save us. No pressure." I went to clink my beer against Lou's water, but he was gone.

"Where *is* Lou?" Teri said.

We scanned the yard. It was nearly dark now, dark enough for the alley light to have come on. Teri went inside and came back out, said, "Nope."

"I'll check the sinkhole," Luke said calmly.

When he said this, I broke into a run. It was my sinkhole. I felt responsible. I got there quickly, but it was empty. The others arrived, and we stood on its periphery, hands on hips.

"The city is sinking," Finn said. "Like Venice."

We looked up and down the street. Luke called for him, loudly.

"I'm going back," Teri said.

Everyone followed. It was a small back yard, fenced, twenty-five yards of space between house and garage. The garage door was cracked, so I moved that way. As soon as I did, I heard piano music. Something familiar and energetic.

"Lou found my piano," I said.

Everyone looked toward the music.

"He's taking lessons," Teri said.

I explained how I'd found it two months ago at the end of a driveway, an old upright. I'd hit a few chords, and an old man ventured out, said he'd tried to sell it in his yard sale the day before, marked it down from $100 to $50 to $25 to $10, then put it on the curb with a "free" sign attached. It had belonged to his dead wife, and he was preparing to move into assisted living. I offered him twenty bucks, but he waved it off. I called Two Men and a Truck—one man with a philosophy degree, the other with a history degree—and they delivered it to my house, carried it up the street around the sinkhole and into the garage. I hated the idea of it going to a landfill. I plunked away all night that first night beneath a single bulb, then stored gas cans on it.

"Jetsam," Finn said.

It was a song anyone should recognize—the Vince Guaraldi "Linus and Lucy" tune from the Charlie Brown Christmas show, the frenetic left hand doing its bass roll for a couple measures before the right hand kicks in with that manic melody that makes every stiff corpse feel like dancing.

"It's out of tune," Finn said.

"The piano has been drinking," I gargled, channeling Tom Waits.

"He played this at his recital last month," Teri said.

"Charles Schultz was manic-depressive," Finn said.

"He got a standing ovation," Luke said.

Maria threw her head from side to side and jogged in place, flapping her arms like Lucy, drunk on the music. I danced in a circle, high-stepping, and soon enough everyone was doing a silly dance. What would a passing group of aliens think, observing this gang of humans move like this on a hot August night as if we were shaking off insects? Maria danced in front of Finn, encouraging him to move, which he began to do, clumsily, without self-consciousness. It may have been his first time dancing. When Lou finished, Finn stepped to the garage.

"Once more, maestro!" he yelled. "Molto allegro!"

Lou obeyed, and we danced again, circling Finn. I didn't care how silly I looked. I wasn't drunk, but it felt like it. Some electric charge hovered and bounced between bodies, and I got lost in the music Lou was making. Maria lifted her arms over her head, and Finn put his hands on her stomach as if to support the bouncing baby. I told myself that I would tell her the following morning how beautiful she looked, how her eyes shined, how the smile Finn returned to her was also oddly beautiful. The air around us turned cool. It was darker now, making the stars more visible, even with the alley light. I didn't want the night to end.

When Lou finished, he came out and we all made a fuss over him.

"It's out of tune," he said, and we all laughed loudly.

In a few minutes, before anyone had time to sit again, Luke said they should call it a night. They needed to get up super-early and drive their rental car to Chicago and catch their plane back to Hawaii.

Teri said, "Finn, where are you staying?" She explained that he had sold his home and gave away everything he owned, keeping only whatever essentials he could fit into his backpack.

"Stay here," I said. "If you'd like to, I mean. We have a foldout couch."

"He can't do air conditioning," Maria reminded me, a little too harshly. "You can have our back yard though, if you'd like it," she said.

"I prefer the riverside," he said. "There is a community there who brag about their waterfront property. But tonight? Yes, I am tired and I will sleep in your yard."

"Okay," I said. "Sure."

"Can we get you anything?" Maria said.

"No, please. I have everything." He pointed to his backpack and the sleeping bag tied to it. Luke, Teri, and Lou took a moment telling Finn goodnight. Luke invited him to Hawaii, and I was not jealous. Maria kissed him on the cheek, and I didn't mind.

We showed Luke, Teri, and Lou to their rooms and went to bed ourselves. Maria went to sleep quickly, and except for a brief dream where our bed turned into a raft that floated down flooded streets, I didn't sleep. I rehashed all the conversations of the evening, wanting to remember every detail. I thought about the life of our child to come, she who would enter the world in another month. I tried to imagine myself evolving into an adult like Luke, Teri, and even Finn, courageous people who were more alive than I.

By 5:30 a.m., the birds were up—the same loud birds that just the day before I'd found annoying, so I gave up on sleep and went downstairs. I looked out front for Luke's rental car and saw that it was gone. I didn't believe I hadn't heard them leave based on how lightly I thought I'd been sleeping. It occurred to me that I might never see them again. I looked out back for Finn, thinking I would take him a cup of coffee, but he too was gone. He'd left no trace of being there at all. I opened a window, felt the soft summer morning, and sat awhile, still without coffee, staring into the back yard full of tiki torches and coolers and fans. I stared at the space where we had danced to Lou's piano. The empty yard was unsettling. I felt an urge to return to our bedroom, to look in on Maria to make certain she was there. Such silly thoughts I had while I stood so still in the middle of the kitchen. I stayed there awhile longer, staring out the window. I wanted to remember that silence and take it with me everywhere.

Love Song for the Headless

Maria had been waiting for an hour in the Pain Manage-ment Clinic waiting room, eager for a refill, hopeful for a higher dose, still bundled in her coat, scarf, gloves, and hat because it was minus forty degrees in Wisconsin, which meant every time someone came shuffling or rolling or crawling through the door, the polar vortex smacked the bullseye painted on her face, and she cursed them. If she had to wait much longer, she'd have to strangle someone. Was chronic pain the leading cause of crime? She didn't want to go to prison. She had a five-year-old son to take care of and a sick husband to nurse back to health and a shit job to avoid being fired from, all while cringing from back spasms that made her want to murder anyone who said (or looked like they *could* say) something agreeable about any of the stupid political leaders who advocated for increased stupidity. Her incompetent doctor said she should learn to live with pain. The second opinion she solicited advised her to be in this waiting room that resembled the purgatory she was no doubt headed toward. So here she was.

From the wall-mounted television, giggling newscasters from the propaganda channel tortured her. Beneath the TV, a two-year-old screamed her little lungs out like a tormented Joplin (Janis, not Scott), while standing on her mother's lap, flapping her arms as if her diaper were on fire. Maria wanted to get in before the kid. She'd arrived first. Were her pain less excruciating—were she not on a time-crunch to pick up Miles—she'd say, "No, please, let the child in ahead of me; I'm happy to suffer longer for her sake." But no, she wanted in first.

An older man sat two seats away, wearing an orange duck-hunting hat, flaps over ears, beard drooping to his chest, newspaper two inches from his eyes. He grunted when he turned the pages. Because they were too heavy? Two elderly women sat across from him wearing matching Green Bay Packers jackets, both eating from bags of popcorn they'd scooped from the machine next to the empty fish tank, talking of yesterday's playoff collapse. They'd come in together, sisters probably, twins maybe, faces blank as tombstones. They kept looking at the screaming baby, kept saying, "Poor baby." The poor baby's mother kept rocking the poor baby, dark eyes set in a ghostly face. Closer to the door, a skinny guy, mid-twenties, bounced his right heel like a jackhammer. He scratched his face with one hand, held his phone in front of his eyes with the other, squeezed it as if it had insulted him.

Maria thought of her mother in Jacksonville, Florida, who one month ago had undergone what was supposed to be a simple kidney procedure to remove a benign tumor, so routine her mother insisted that Maria shouldn't come home. Her mother had said, "Don't worry about *me*, honey, you have enough to feel guilty about." So she focused her guilt on being a bad mom and bad wife, a failing teacher and cold colleague, an apathetic neighbor, passive citizen, pill addict, a selfish only child who couldn't fly home to hold her mother's hand before she went into surgery and to assure her that she'd be there when they wheeled her back out.

Today, she felt guilty for feeling good about canceling her classes. She hated the gen-ed students who hated the music they were required to appreciate, and she hated herself for being mean to them for hating it. She wanted to stop her colleagues in the hall, explain that her back pain made it difficult to smile these days, ask them what sort of pain *they* were learning to live with and how did they manage it? Her mother told her last month, via telephone, to "offer it up," which was what she'd told Maria in her youth every time she fell out of a tree, or off a bike, or got whacked in the head with a softball she was supposed to catch. Marty too had been saying, "Please. Find a therapist." And just this morning, finally, to herself, she'd said, *okay, yes,* and following her Pain Management appointment, she intended to step next door and make an appointment with Dr. R. Angle, PhD, certified psychologist.

But it was already 4:30, and she had to pick up Miles from his new preschool before five and didn't want to embarrass him by being late. He'd gotten kicked out of his last preschool for punching three other kids on three separate days, allegedly unprovoked, and with no explanation afterward from Miles, which led to weekly appointments with a child therapist who was having no better luck getting him to talk than Maria and Marty were having. Medications were being discussed, debated, fought over.

The bearded man said, "Fake news," turned a page, grunted. The baby's screams were operatic, amplified, off-key. The Packer sisters took turns saying, "Poor baby."

It'd be easier to live with pain if she still lived in Florida, away from a landlocked state and its bland food and gray skies. She preferred an occasional hurricane over living inside a freezer. And she'd prefer not to summarize her life every time she said hello and revealed her accent and got the inevitable "Where are *you* from?"

Over the screaming baby, one Packer sister told the other, "Ted Stein has been brain-dead for a month yet after slipping on the ice, still hooked to the machines, poor thing, and his children never call him."

"Poor thing," her sister said.

With a dose of stronger meds, Maria might manage a good night's sleep. She might wake up restored, might return to the treadmill for a mile, might enter the campus-wide meeting addressing budget cuts and layoffs without a sense of panic, even as she knew the music department would be the first to go. Following that meeting, she might very well find the old spring in her step and waltz, as she once did, into the auditorium to greet one hundred hearing-impaired sophomores whose collective angst was impossible to pierce, even last week when she veered from the syllabus and played Hendrix playing "The Star-Spangled Banner," at which point students grimaced and poked fingers into ears. One said, "But wasn't he on drugs?" And just like that, she veered again, suggesting *they* try drugs. Then she riffed through a lecture on the history of psychedelic music, played a sample of the fifth movement of Hector Berlioz's "Symphonie Fantastique" (1830), written while Hector enjoyed opium, then she sped through the heroin-infused jazz of the '20s, trying, before class ended, to reach the Beatles, then the Merry Pranksters and the cultural conditions of those times that fed the music and fueled rebellion. The students grew sleepy, despite all the Red Bull in the room. After an hour, and still with twenty minutes to go, she said, "Fuck it," and let them go, which cued the cacophonous unzipping and rezipping of backpacks, sounds that made Maria's brain dance with apoplectic rage.

The office phone kept ringing, an old-timey bell-ringing rotary phone, circa 1976, that bounced off the hollow walls, inducing a migraine in Maria to complement her back pain. At the first meeting with the pain management specialist, she'd said, "I also have chronic misophonia." He typed that into his records and said, "What's that?" A strong sensitivity, she explained, to certain sounds that might, if severe enough, trigger a desire to kill whoever's making the noise. When Miles attacked his cereal bowl with his spoon, for example, or when people ate popcorn with their mouths open, or men grunted while reading newspapers, or kids shook the walls because they bounced their heels, or pedantic pundits praised a racist devil, making babies scream. She looked at her phone again. Nothing. She inhaled deeply. Closed her eyes.

She'd hurt her back shoveling too much snow too fast because she was late for work and needed to dig out her car. Since then, a year ago, she'd twice fallen on ice, spraining her back. She hated to think they'd grow old while walking over ice, breaking arms, hips, necks. Marty kept saying, "It could be worse." Before he got exhausted from being sick, he stayed exhausted from working third shift at the hospital, cleaning rooms vacated by the dead, mopping up urine and vomit and blood, cleaning toilets, wiping down every sur-face a human could breathe upon, talking to ghosts, staying invisible himself to the nurses who ignored him as they stepped around his cart. When Maria complained about her job, he said, "What do you do again? Listen to music? Talk about music?"

Worse than the ringing phone was the overly chipper tone-deaf receptionist just home from the set of *Fargo* with her vowels that pierced her script like ice picks: "It's $\underline{A}$ *beau-tee*-ful *more*-ning at Weee-Care pAIn clin*ic*, h*ow* can we ease *your* pain today?"

The baby screamed. The baby's mother looked toward the ringing phone. A Packer sister said, "Sounds like she's being tortured, poor thing."

The bearded man flapped his paper. "Torture?" he said. "You want to talk about torture?"

Maria didn't want to talk about torture. She stared at her silent phone, looking through it all the way to her mother's incision.

"I'll tell you about torture," he said. He lowered his paper, looked at Maria as if *she'd* made the comment. "Every six weeks, I get a shot in each eye because I got doused with napalm in Vietnam. I've had a headache since 1965. But them's the breaks when you fight for freedom. I knew what I was signing up for."

Maria laughed, a reflex as quick as a hammer to the knee. She pictured him carrying a machine gun through a Vietnamese jungle while wearing his orange duck-hunting hat. He looked at her, and she looked away. She knew engaging him would lead to greater pain, a kind of torture. She knew better than to say anything at all.

She said, "Aren't you angry that you were sent into an unwinnable war?"

"The media lost that war," he said, and flapped his small-town daily to illustrate what the media looked like. He looked at the Packer sisters for affirmation, and they nodded while chewing, though Maria wasn't sure they'd heard him over the screaming baby. She wanted to yank the newspaper out of his hands and rip it into shreds. She decided to say nothing else. Anything else would create more tension that would escalate, turn hostile. She stared through the front glass and looked forward to stepping into the freezer that waited for her.

She wanted to call Marty, say, "I'm sorry." She wanted to call her dead father in purgatory, say, "Sorry I didn't call you more often. See you soon." She wanted to call her mother, say, "Sorry, sorry, sorry," one thousand times in a row.

A worker in white stepped out with a clipboard. She was in her twenties, but prematurely old, more exhausted and dead-eyed than anyone in the waiting room. For one second Maria saw the toll it took to deal with people in pain, and she wanted to apologize to her too.

The worker called the mother with the screaming baby.

"I was here first," Maria mumbled.

"Here's what I want to know," the bearded man announced. "With all the beheadings going on over there, what are we doing for all the people who've had their heads cut off?"

Maria laughed again, more explosively.

He stared at her, like, "What's wrong with you?" The Packer sisters looked curious too. She wanted to ask if he knew the success rates for head-reattachment procedures or whether first-aid for the headless had ever helped.

He said, "You're not from around here, are you? Got an accent, sounds like." He narrowed his eyes to get a better look at the affliction around her mouth.

Sometimes it was a harmless "Where are you from?" conversation-starter. Other times, the passive-aggressive MO of the Midwest announced itself like the shadow of a shark fin and all Maria heard was: "You're not one of us." She'd heard it from real estate agents, neighbors, bankers, dentists, even professors. Professors were the worst, sneering with smug assumptions about everyone from a red state, making a caricature of the dialect anytime they wanted to imitate someone saying something stupid.

Maria said, "You have an accent too."

He cocked his head like a confused chicken. The Packer sisters watched, awaiting escalation. Maria needed to retreat, soften up, disarm, or the teaching moment was lost.

"I'm from a small town in Florida," she said. "I came here for work five years ago. It's a pretty place." To pacify a native anywhere, Maria knew, compliment their home. The office phone went off again and the receptionist recited her script again.

"You people," the man said. "You're still fighting the Civil War down there."

The Packer sisters eyed Maria, looking for her musket. The guy in the corner looked up too, in case the musket was concealed. And the truth—the *sad* truth, (a truth she'd confess to Dr. R. Angle, certified) was this: she wanted to retrieve the hatchet-handle she kept beneath her driver's seat. She'd learned this from her grandfather, who kept a handle beneath his truck seat, which he called his n-word knocker, a phrase that nauseated her then and filled her with great shame now. But he was indiscriminate—he waved it at anyone who pulled too far past red lights. She'd lifted her own handle only once, while cursing a driver who rolled through a four way stop. Miles had been with her, so she made it a teaching moment. "Be courteous of other drivers," she had said. "Be *kind*," she said.

The bearded man said, "You people never surrendered."

Maria imagined waving her hatchet-handle around the waiting room, first at the man, then at the receptionist and her phone. But she surrendered. She leaned forward, stretched her back, closed her eyes and inhaled deeply.

"I went to Disney World thirty years ago," the man said. "Stopped at a gas station in Georgia, Confederate flags waving everywhere, then I went inside, saw these old men standing around talking, so I said hello and they asked me, said did I know the difference between a damned Yankee and a goddamned Yankee, and they said it's one who's visiting versus one who's staying. So I said to my wife, 'so much for that southern hospitality you hear about.'"

The Packer sisters looked at Maria so she could answer for this crime, maybe make reparations. And she *wanted* to apologize, to say that unkindness wasn't right there or any-where. Instead, she retaliated with her own story, said, "Last Sunday, I was shoveling snow, and this guy stopped by with a snowblower, offered to do my sidewalk for ten bucks. I asked him if he wouldn't rather be watching the Packers, and he said, 'No, I don't care nothing about watching a bunch of'— and then he used the n-word. I told him to leave." This last part wasn't true. She'd waited for him to finish the sidewalk, gave him ten bucks, and spent a sleepless night preparing the lengthy lecture she would excoriate him with next time.

"You know what the guy said?" Maria said. "He said, 'You're not from around here, are you?'" That part was true.

"Was he driving a green truck?" the man said.

"He didn't care about the Packers?" one woman said.

"If it was a green truck, it was my neighbor, Brock. He's not hitting on all cylinders."

The office phone rang.

"I wish he'd come by *our* house," her sister said.

"Not if he's a Bears fan," the other said.

The phone rang again.

The worker in white stepped out and called the guy in the corner who limped across the room, head down.

"I was here first," Maria mumbled.

"Brock's from Missouri," the man said. "A southern state."

It's a beautiful morning

"Isn't Missouri in the Midwest?" one woman said.

at We-care Pain Management clinic.

"Missouri's the south," the man said. "They owned slaves there. Ask Mark Twain."

How can we ease your pain today?

"Missouri's in the Southeastern Conference," the other woman said. "With Alabama, Georgia, Florida. Teams like that."

"But that arch-looking thing in St. Louis," her sister said. "You're supposed to go through that to head west—what's it called?"

"Excuse me," Maria said. She stood and stepped toward the door to fetch her hatchet. Then a worker stepped out again and called the bearded man, who got up slowly, made a show of shaking his head (*some people*, his head said) while he gathered his coat, grimaced and grunted, and left Maria alone with the Packer sisters, who looked away. It was 4:45. The TV talking heads talked more loudly about the dangers of immigrants.

"The arch," a Packer sister said. "It's called the arch. In St. Louis."

"That's right," her sister said. "You go through that to go west."

The worker in white came back, called the name of one woman, so both women rose and went in together, one for support, no doubt, a good listener who would take notes, a team, which suddenly made Maria jealous. She turned off the TV.

A minute later, the mother came out carrying her baby, whose head was propped on her mother's shoulder, eyes closed, having received a shot of the good stuff. They went through the door, letting in cold air. The younger guy came out, stared at his phone while marching toward the door and through it, letting in cold air. It was 4:55. The bearded man came out, limped to the door without acknowledging Maria, face like cement, and went through the door, letting in cold air. The Packer sisters came next, zipped their coats and walked out, talking of their efficient visit. The receptionist turned off the lights.

"Hey," Maria said.

She turned the lights back on.

"Oh," she said. "Didn't see you there."

Maria approached the window, gave her name. "I was here at 3:30, for my 3:30 appointment that was scheduled today *for 3:30*."

The lady looked at her calendar. "Did you check in?"

She hadn't checked in.

"I'm sorry," the lady said. "There must've been a mix-up."

"Yes, obviously, you made a mix-up."

She flipped a page. "I see you here, *tomorrow* at four o'clock."

That couldn't be right. She was out of pills. "I'm out of pills," she said.

"I'm sorry. If you can make it—"

"Can we call—I'm sure you have a cell number for someone."

"No," she said. "I can't do that." She'd replaced her chipper telephone voice with the disciplinarian voice she used on her children seventy years ago. She stared at Maria with jail-warden eyes. Maria squeezed the ledge outside the lady's window. She wanted to release the ledge and grab a chair she could throw. She'd thrown lots of things in her mother's house while she went through high school, and her mother came home to find her house in shambles, a single mom working jobs she hated to pay for a house Maria wanted to destroy. Dr. R. Angle might say, *Is that where your guilt begins?* and Maria might answer, *Shut up.* Dr. R. Angle might follow with *Where was your father? Tell me about your father*, and Maria might walk out.

She'd have to get through the night with something else, call first thing in the morning. Her brain made a strange noise. She smelled mold or mildew or swamp gas. Her stomach lining burned. She turned away, stepped into the freezing dark—so dark so early now with such short cloudy days—and let the cold air slap her face. Her car was a cold casket. But there were seat warmers and she'd have Miles's seat warm for him before he climbed in. She'd gone in debt for seat warmers. She'd bought a new SUV to get through unplowed alleys, her first-ever new car, which she felt guilty for admiring. She inspected it daily to make sure the doors weren't dinged.

It was 5:11. Miles stood outside, waiting. They'd locked the doors at five, he said, and left because he'd sworn his mother was coming.

"Those assholes couldn't wait with you for five minutes?" He'd stop shivering soon, she knew; the car was warm, his seat was warm.

Miles slumped and sulked, deepened his silent treatment. They drove to the grocery store in silence, but she was about to tell him he could get whatever he wanted. Another pizza for dinner? She'd have beer. She called her mother.

The parking lot was packed, of course, with the after-work mob. She drove down two aisles, stopped so a hundred-year-old man could hobble by. Another car sat on her bumper, waiting for her and the car ahead. Her mother's phone was ringing. At the end of the next aisle, Miles said, "Uh-Oh." To their right, moving backwards out of a parking space toward Miles's door: a Buick. Maria tapped her horn. The person ahead of her raised a middle finger. Her mother's phone was ringing. The Buick kept coming. Maria held her horn for a four count, loud enough for a deaf person to hear in Canada. The Buick was going to hit her new car. She was going to have to stand in the cold and argue over blame, wait for a cop, trade insurance info. She held the horn. Miles scooted toward the middle to escape injury.

The Buick hit Miles's door and made a *thunk* louder than Maria expected. Miles yelped like a little girl and Maria hung up her phone, turned off her car, reached beneath her seat for her hatchet handle. It wasn't there. All at once, she concluded that Miles had told his father about it, and he'd taken it, put it in his divorce file. This pissed her off more than the deaf Buick driver. She reached behind her for Miles's big plastic bat. It'd been there for six months, the fat end of it big as a cartoon bat, which made it hard to miss a ball, though Miles managed to miss every time, and the last time they'd gone to the park, Maria had grown impatient at his consistent whiffs from five feet until Miles finally said, "I hate you."

She grabbed the bat and went out and around her car, through the headlights of the car behind her. She raised the bat over her head with both hands and slammed it on the Buick's trunk six consecutive times, feeling no pain. So she did it again. Then again. Then she carried it to the driver's door, waiting for it to open so she could start swinging. She crouched into the batter's stance of a right-handed power-hitter, teeth clenched, ready to send a human head into orbit. Behind Maria, the car that had been on her bumper sped away. When the Buick door opened, finally, slowly, the tip of a cane came poking out. A skinny leg followed.

A second skinny leg followed the first, two skinny legs now straddling a cane held by a ninety-year-old woman.

Maria lowered her bat, feeling sick to her stomach. The old woman pulled herself out of the car and leaned on her cane. She was the height of Maria's mother, 5'1. They had the same gray hair—a short tight perm her mother got every Wednesday at 9 a.m. The parking spot the woman had tried to pull back into was a handicapped space she'd missed again. The woman looked into Maria's eyes. She didn't mention the terrible noise Maria had made on her trunk. She didn't mention how her car had backed into Maria's. Her eyes were milky gray, like Maria's mother's eyes when she was tired. The old woman didn't acknowledge Maria's bat or ask what she planned to do with it. She pointed toward her open door.

"Do you know how to raise those seats?" she said. "It's my husband's car. He died last year and I'm out of bologna."

"I'm so sorry," Maria said, thinking of what she had come so close to doing.

"He never liked bologna, but I do. One must go on, mustn't one?"

She wanted to hug the old lady, to cry on her shoulder, to ask forgiveness, to take her home. She sat in the lady's car, fiddled with the manual adjustments, moved the seat backwards and forwards, backwards and forwards, backwards and forwards, but not *up*. There was no way to move it *up*. She tried until her hands grew too cold to work. She got out and faced her, still holding her bat, looked deeply into her eyes. She said, "I'm sorry. I can't—I don't know."

"My daughter will fix it," the woman said. "She stops by every day after work to check on me. Such a good girl." Then she walked away, leaving her car door open. Maria closed it for her, returned to her car, placed the bat in the back seat. Miles was silent. More deeply silent than ever after watching his mother behave like a deranged lunatic. Maybe he'd grow up to repeat the story to therapists and friends: "The day my mother wanted to kill an elderly woman." She imagined then a scenario where the driver had been a man with a gun who would've shot her dead while Miles watched. Her back hurt now, more than it had all day, and her hands were dumb blocks of wood, shaking. She rested her forehead on the wheel and started the car.

"We're okay," she said. "I'm sorry. I just need to call Grandma." She was crying now as she stopped to wave one car ahead of her. She said, "Siri, call Mom."

"Mom?" Miles said.

"We're okay," she said. She kept driving and didn't wipe her face. Her mother's phone was ringing again. Maria would quit the pills cold turkey. She'd learn to live with pain, like her first doctor said she should. She'd offer it up, as her mother advised.

"One must go on," she told Miles.

"But Mom," Miles said.

New snow had started falling, which she hated to see because it meant more shoveling. She waited for her mother to answer her ringing phone.

"Mom," Miles said. "Gramma died last month."

She looked at Miles to see how serious he was. He seemed to know. She remembered then, and laughed while crying, then cried harder. Then laughed at the logic of forgetting. She saw herself sitting in the front row of her mother's ancient church, Miles next to her, too young for a funeral, Marty on her other side, squeezing her hand. The church where Maria had received her first communion, given her first (and last) confession, had been confirmed. She faced the ten-foot wax figure of Jesus stretched out on real wood, thorny crown-capped head hanging to one side, sword-wound to the ribs, naked but for a skinny towel, knobby knees and all, hanging there front and center as a favor for the visually (and spiritually) impaired. She remembered the old organ in the balcony hitting fat chords that floated over the church and hummed inside her bones.

She was crying so hard now she had to stop at the edge of the parking lot. She cried until Miles said what he said next.

He said, "Maybe I should drive."

He found a Kleenex and passed it to her. "Yes," she said. "I think you should."

She moved slowly through the falling snow toward home, thinking she'd warm some soup for dinner, take a bowl to bed-bound Marty and place it outside his door. She turned up the Berlioz and drove slowly, both hands on the wheel, eyes fixed where her headlights stopped. She heard something new in the final movement then, as if an eleven-fingered pianist were reaching new ghost notes, as discernible as the wind from a conductor's wand, as vital as the space between heartbeats.

"Listen to that," Maria said.

He was listening. She knew he heard it too. She knew his eyes were closed, that he was listening hard, that he was hearing what others wouldn't. They went the rest of the way without talking, Berlioz between them, telling them to linger, to have a little faith that this field of colors blossoming strangely in the music now would keep them company through the night and through all the difficult and beautiful years to come.

The Enormous Typewriter

At 5 a.m. they heard a crash like a house had fallen from the sky, so Marty told Maria, "We're fine, everything's fine." He fought to untangle his feet and find the floor and sprint down the hall to their six-year-old, Miles, so he could tell *him* that everything was fine. Miles had only recently started sleeping in his own bed, with a flashlight, but kept returning to their bed because of little noises or not enough noises. Marty had trouble kicking off the sheets. He imagined a cartoon character running in place, no hero at all, useless to his family. He remembered the previous night's tornado warning (in Wisconsin, in September) and Maria's worry that bad weather would disrupt the important day ahead of them that they'd posted on the calendar two months ago after a local doctor referred them to a specialist in Rochester (an hour's drive) who would take a better look at the peculiar spot inside Miles's brain.

Maria was already inside Miles's room, of course, even before she knew the source of the sound. Marty, meanwhile, had reached the bedroom window. Their biggest tree, the one that had been leaning for three years, had fallen across the driveway, barely missing the house. A great relief, as Marty saw it. He took his first deep breath and went to share the good news.

Miles had pulled his blanket over his head. "Are we about to die?" he said.

"No one's dying," Marty said. "It was just a tree. Let's go back to sleep."

"Come to our bed," Maria said.

Normally, Marty would question the soundness of this idea, whether it reinforced the child's belief that he should keep being rescued, but that was a dumb thought today.

Miles climbed out of bed clinging to his stuffed fish, Marlin. He said, "I have a headache."

"I know you do," Maria said. "It'll be better soon."

Back in their bedroom, Marty pulled the curtain back. "See," he said. "Just a tree." It was still dark, but the corner streetlight flickered, wind-blown limbs fanning across it, treetops dancing. There was no rain, no tornado. Only wind. And one giant tree, lying vertically.

Miles climbed into the middle of their bed, hugging Marlin.

Maria, still at the window, put her palms on her face and produced a little sob that pierced Marty's heart. "It's blocking the car," she said. "We need to leave in six hours."

"No problem," Marty said.

"It *is* a problem," she said. "*This*—" and she stopped herself.

He was glad she didn't say what she was thinking, that for the past three years she'd been saying he should call a tree-person (an "arborist," was her term) to ask if the tree was rotting and if they couldn't save it, have it removed before it fell on the house or across the driveway and blocked their only car, which, who knows, maybe they'd need for a fucking emergency some day. Marty had studied the angles. Even *if* it fell (which it wouldn't do soon, *he* said), the longest limbs would miss the house by six feet. Part of him wanted credit for being right about that, but the smarter part of him knew he shouldn't ask for it.

"I knew it would miss the house," he said.

She grunted, a sound of exhaustion. She said, "Get it moved. Handle it. Call someone." She returned to bed, said something soft to Miles that Marty couldn't hear.

He went to the kitchen, turned on the coffee. Call someone? No. He'd take care of it. He wanted to prove to himself and to his family that he could be counted on at a time like this. He'd restore order, establish calm on this stressful day. Their local doctor had said, "I don't know. It's a curious mass." He kept telling Maria it would be fine—those Mayo docs are the best in the business at curious masses—but she couldn't hear it. And now the tree. A big tree. He was generally hopeless with home repair projects beyond lightbulb replacement and the routine cleaning chores associated with his job as a third-shift custodian at the hospital. But he owned an electric chainsaw. Never used. And a long extension cord. Somewhere. How difficult could a chainsaw be? There was time. Plenty of time to clear enough space for the car.

He sipped coffee, read the morning newsfeed from his phone. No mention of tornadoes, but a new hurricane spun toward the Florida coast to his mother's house and his childhood bedroom. An earthquake in Turkey killed 19,000, a mudslide in Sierra Leone had buried hundreds. California was on fire again. Firefighters were being shot. Nigeria was drowning. The President bragged that the U.S. nuclear arsenal was locked and loaded, ready to unleash with fire and fury should anyone be man enough to challenge him to a duel. Over the weekend, white nationalists had gathered in Charlottesville, one of whom drove his car into a crowd of protesters, murdering Heather Heyer, thirty-two, who was promoting peace. "Sick times," Marty said aloud. He read the news until 7 a.m., hopeful Maria and Miles were sleeping, worried a chainsaw would disturb them, his neighbors. There was time.

He gave himself a pep talk: he was forty, not too young and not too old for the job. If necessary, he'd summon the strength to lift the tree with his own bare hands and hurl it to the side if that's what it took to get Miles to Rochester. He went to his closet. Pulled out his long-sleeve flannel, imagined himself a lumberjack. He stretched to loosen the back he'd injured last winter shoveling snow. In the garage, he searched for his safety goggles. Found them beside the chainsaw, still unused. He went inside for his lens-cleaner, wiped his regular glasses, then his safety goggles, then slipped the goggles over his glasses. He found the Pro-Grade safety earmuffs (noise reduction rating 34 db) he'd bought three years ago to muffle *neighbors'* chainsaws, mowers, leaf blowers. Dropped his like-new work gloves on the concrete, relaced his stiff hiking boots, then stepped on the gloves to kill nesting spiders (a trick learned from Maria). When he opened the garage door, he saw only tree, no street. No problem. He plugged one end of his extension cord into the garage wall outlet, unrolled it to the driveway as far as it would go, plugged the other end into his chainsaw, which, he noticed now, was more of a limb trimmer. The sky, peppered with dark clouds, said *go*. He looked at his phone to ascertain the conditions. Windy and forty-five degrees.

He should've called someone. Was it an ash like those being removed across the city because of an infestation? When had Maria not known best? Or a cedar? Should he start at the top? Maybe a maple. Or the bottom? It was *not* a pine. He knew a pine when he saw a pine. If someone were to ask him whether this tree was a pine, he'd say *no*, it was certainly not a pine.

Five minutes later, Maria walked out with Miles, who was hugging his fish. They stared at the tree, awed by its size. The wind blew their hair, and Maria folded her arms across her chest. Marty went to hug them, to say everything was fine.

"Everything's fine," he said.

"Please," Maria said. "Don't hug people while you're holding a chainsaw."

They faced the tree. The tallest part was a foot taller than Marty, who was 5' 9¼", though he wasn't above stretching this truth on official forms, even after Maria, a truth-stickler, corrected him, an act he perceived (defensively, she suggested) as part of a life-long pattern of people selling him short.

To Miles, he said, "We're lucky this tree fell when it did. Think of the firewood."

"Too green for this winter," Maria said. She was smarter about everything, and Marty was grateful she stayed with him. He cursed himself for not having already stocked up on firewood. But there was time.

"Start at the top," she said, and pointed so he'd know. "Make small pieces that won't be too heavy. Stay focused. Don't get distracted like you do."

"No problem," he said. Had he forgotten breakfast? His stomach said so. Maria looked at him in a way that made him sympathize with her and women like her, who looked at men like him in a way that said *why must you insist on acting as if you know what you're doing?*

Miles lifted Marlin toward his mouth and practiced his ventriloquism. "Don't get distracted," Marlin said.

"Your lips were moving," Marty said.

Maria grabbed Miles's hand and led him toward the street. Marty thought: *where are you going, my reasons for living, and what if you don't return, and how should I just this second say I'm willing to cut off both my legs if it should mean no harm will come to either of you?*

"Hey!" he said. "Where are you going?"

"Swimming lessons," Maria shouted. "It's Monday."

"That's right," Marty said, like he'd known. The Y was .06 miles away, an unpleasant hike this morning down sidewalks littered with downed limbs and dead leaves, wind in their faces, black sky pressing down. Ahead of them, Joe, their neighbor, limped along with his cane, rehabbing his leg. Three months ago, he'd been riding his bicycle with his two kids when he got into an altercation with the driver of a truck at a red light, yelling at the driver that he was violating the three feet of space law, prompting the driver to run over his bicycle. And his foot.

Three dogs ran wild. Another was half-visible inside an overblown garbage can. A truck beeped while backing up and someone fed a woodchipper, a sound Marty heard as skeletons being pulverized. He saw Miles push his fingers into his ears, Marlin tucked in the crook of his arm. Maria moved into the wind, arms folded, chin pointed down. Marty wanted to run after them, take them bigger coats, give Miles his ear protection.

Miles took swimming lessons from someone named Chris that Maria was always talking about. *That Chris,* she'd say, *is so good at making him brave.* Which made Marty jealous. Shouldn't *he* be making Miles brave? Was Maria sleeping with Chris? Silly. Was Marty so insecure that his paranoid thoughts bloomed into movies featuring Chris and Maria having sex in chlorinated pools? Yes. What he wanted was to be the kind of man who would solve the tree crisis and drive his son and wife to the Mayo in Rochester, modeling courage all the way.

He started at the bottom. Deep into his first incision, his limb trimmer got stuck. He went for the unused axe he'd bought in April, back when he'd planned on devoting the summer to stocking up on firewood, thinking he'd fell the dead trees that filled the woodsy back yard. Maria liked the sounds and smells and light of the fires, and Marty liked making them, maintaining them, feeling responsible for keeping his family warm during soul-freezing nights.

After his third swing, he stopped, curious about a strange new noise that sounded like an electric typewriter, amplified. When he removed his earmuffs, the typewriter got louder, even with the woodchipper in the distance. It was *above* him, as if coming from a cloud. The typist's eight fingers blazed away, each key punching the cartridge with percussive clarity, steady bass-hum beneath it all, like a motor. Marty knew the sound. It was like the electric IBM he'd inherited from his grandmother that he'd first heard while lying in her bed, sick with fever, she at her corner desk, typing deep into the night while he dreamed of manic drummers. *That* sound was *this* sound, magnified. He needed to know that others heard it too.

Mick, his neighbor to the left, whose yard signs supported the idiot racist the white nationalists loved, stood in his yard holding a beer, headlamp still strapped around his head. He was seventy-something, a Vietnam war vet, retired long-haul trucker who now drove a newspaper route. They'd stopped speaking the day Mick planted his yard signs. When they were speaking, he told Marty he never slept. Now, Marty stepped toward him, yelled, "Hey!"

"You coming to murder me?" Mick said.

Marty's axe was propped over his left shoulder. He liked the feel of it there. He pointed to the sky, said, "You hear that?"

"That chopper's been circling for a half-hour, man."

There *was* a circling helicopter, Marty noticed then, which drowned out the woodchipper when it got right overhead, but the typewriter pierced through them both. Every few weeks, a helicopter circled the surrounding bluffs searching for wounded, lost, or dead hikers. The wounded hikers often fell or rolled a few hundred feet after taking selfies, then used the phones they'd never released to call 911.

"No," Marty said. "It's like a giant typewriter. It's—"

"Sorry about your tree," Mick said. "You need a beer?"

The beer was tempting, but not the company. It was time to hold people accountable for their destructive votes. Marty had told Miles to ignore Mick, then he told Maria they should move. Since the election, in their neighborhood alone, bricks were hurled through windows, the n-word was spray-painted across one door, a swastika across another. A yoga instructor had dumped a box of nails in Mick's driveway, which Mick caught on his home-security cameras, and he pressed charges. The first and only time Marty accepted a beer, Mick told him he and his wife were drowning in medical bills, but didn't reveal from what. He shared he had a son who didn't speak to him, but didn't say why. He shared that his father had—and he put a finger to his head and cocked his thumb. He talked of his time in the Marines.

"No," Marty said to the current beer offer. "I just wondered if you heard that—"

"How's your poetry going?" Mick asked. He once asked Marty what he liked to do in his spare time, and when Marty told him he liked to write poetry, Mick raised his eyebrows in a way that reminded Marty of high school, when a jock named John Keller called him faggot-fingers because Marty liked to play the beat up piano in the school's practice room after lunch.

Marty squeezed his axe handle. "There's a lot to write about these days."

The helicopter circled, the woodchipper ate its skeletons, and the typewriter typed paradiddles. He gave Mick a cold stare. If he wanted to get into it, Marty was ready to get into it. Mick's headlamp shined into Marty's eyes, so it was hard to look through his yellow-tinted glasses to see if anyone was home in there.

"That's for sure," Mick said. "Everything's been upside down since Barbara died. I feel like writing a long-ass poem myself."

Barbara? His wife? Had Marty known? Had Maria?

"I'm trying to join her if I could just kill my liver." He laughed at himself, lifted his beer in a mock toast, and finished it. "In the meantime, I'm just trying to keep a roof over my head. You want to borrow my chainsaw to get your fingernail file unstuck?"

Marty thought: you poor fucker; you've been on a beer-only diet so long, your brain is soup. And grief, that indefatigable bastard, is killing you. The typewriter *click-clacked*. Marty looked down the street, saw the lone black woman in the neighborhood (as far as he knew), he'd met years earlier, a woman with two grandchildren whose door had been spray-painted. She was dragging a limb to the street. He wanted to help, to ask if *she* heard the enormous typewriter.

To his back, Mick said, "Good luck, amigo."

A red party balloon flapped on the corner lot, the property next to Mick's where a house had been vacant for three years without so much as a for-sale sign. The balloon was tied to something solid between the sidewalk and the street. When he got closer, he saw the balloon said, "Get Well Soon!" It was tied to the neck of a dead squirrel. When Marty pictured Miles and Maria passing it, he felt like vomiting. He wanted to hunt down the sick fuck who had done this so he could swing his axe at them. He picked the squirrel up by its tail so they wouldn't see it on their way home, and carried it down the street, axe propped on one shoulder, balloon bouncing in the wind. The woman had dropped her limb in the street, looked at him while she brushed her hands together, then shook her head and quickly walked away.

The typewriter hung in the dark sky, keys blazing.

Joe rounded the corner again, moving quickly with his cane, and when he spotted Marty, he veered sharply toward the opposite sidewalk, kept moving. Marty called after him, jogged to catch up. Joe stopped, pressed a button on his watch, turned to face Marty. The wind blew the Get Well balloon between them, hitting Joe's nose. Marty admired Joe. His wife had left him shortly after the man in the truck ran over his foot, had taken their two kids with her. But here he was, enduring this harsh world with courage, limping along to regain his strength, which oddly made Marty jealous. Did Marty possess such strength? He doubted it. Joe lifted a bloody handkerchief toward his blood-coated mustache. The blood had dripped from his nose, painting his white mustache red. He looked like he'd just eaten a gazelle. He dabbed it again, looked at Marty's squirrel, then his axe.

"Why are you killing squirrels, Marty?" he said.

"Do you hear that typewriter?"

"All I hear are my allergies. And a sinus headache. Or a brain tumor."

He was trying to be funny. He didn't know. He said, "I have to walk fifty-two more minutes." He pressed his watch, pushed his cane ahead and followed it, waving his bloody handkerchief over his shoulder.

Marty stood there with his squirrel and his balloon, axe over one shoulder. The enormous typewriter came from the trees. Down the center of the next street, a young girl walked a goat who wore a pink sweater. "Good morning," Marty said. She led her goat to the opposite sidewalk, quickened her pace, and said to her goat, "Don't worry."

What his grandmother had been writing that night she typed all night while he lay sick in her bed was her last will and testament. He missed that bed. He had yet to find a bed as comfortable. She told him she was about to die and she wanted a clear record of her last wishes. He'd asked to see what she was writing, and she'd okay, but only when she'd finished. Then she pushed her chair back, said she was going for a Tab Cola and a cigarette, made Marty promise he wouldn't look when she left the room. Then he looked. Couldn't make sense of it. She caught him looking, said, "You break your promise, I keep mine." She typed into the night and Marty fell asleep to the noise. The next morning he saw no sign of her last wishes. Neither of them mentioned it. Six months later, after her funeral, Marty's mother set the heavy typewriter on his bedroom desk. The last line of his grandmother's will said, "Give Marty my typewriter."

He heard the train, which reminded him of the mayor, who lived across the tracks. The bells and lights went off and the arms came down, so he walked between them, axe over shoulder, squirrel in hand. Was the typewriter coming from the mayor's house? If the mayor was home, Marty planned to ask him why he so often praised the snake-eyed governor: a college-dropout who inherited his millions and hated poor people for the threats they posed. He hoped the mayor read his letter to the editor that expressed opposition to the second line of tracks which now ran parallel to the first, installed at haste so oil-owners and RR magnates could increase production from sacred Native American land in North Dakota and maximize distribution to New York, doubling the chances of derailments that would kill water supplies and ruin wildlife, which was the same story repeated since the 1880s (Marty wrote in his letter) when millionaires monopolized supply laws that increased their wealth while keeping poor laborers poor, which the God-loving rich pricks deemed the Christian thing to do.

The train blew past. Marty counted sixty-eight oil-tankers. When the train faded, the typewriter emerged again. He smelled a strong cigar, traced it to the nearest driveway where an old man in overalls sat in a wheelchair, hooking one end of an air compressor to the groin-area of the inflatable Packer-player who'd had the wind knocked out of him. His house was painted a dull shade of green and gold manufactured in 1966, matching mailbox. On the stoop of the next house sat an unattended suitcase, and on the roof of its neighbor, a baby stroller. Marty looked again. Yes, baby stroller on the roof. He continued with his dead squirrel and his axe toward the corner tavern, entertained the idea of slipping in for a quick one as he did on some of his late-evening insomnia-inspired strolls. Then he saw the yellow tape circling the building and remembered what he'd read last week: two men in their eighties had been talking politics through happy hour, then a poke led to a punch, which led to floor-wrestling, which led to a fatal gunshot still under investigation. The shooter concealed a pistol in one pocket, carried his concealed carry permit in the other. When concealed carry passed, Marty wrote a letter he called *Give Guns to Drunk People Only*, which prompted 103 violent comments and twenty-three direct threats. Then he wrote another letter titled *The Age of No Reason*, which prompted 180 hateful comments and thirty-five threats. Then he stopped writing letters. He seethed instead, went sleepless longer.

Across the street, the Catholic church's front door was open. Marty had attended one mass there (a curious Mass) three years ago, a December when he'd felt some desperate nostalgia for the old Florida church (built in 1835) his grandmother took him to and where he'd served briefly as an altar boy before being fired for daydreaming. This church felt like a fast-food restaurant. The priest had promised to finish up before kickoff, then lifted his robe to reveal his Packers jersey. Afterwards, Marty went to the tavern across the street, got in line for a beer, saw the priest ahead of him, then turned around and walked out, favoring a long walk through the woods, where the trees talked of silence.

He rang the mayor's doorbell. And forgot why. What had he wanted to say? "Is this your squirrel?" He turned from the stoop, looked at the gray-black sky. The typewriter sounded softer, but it had not slowed. The mayor wasn't home. Marty dropped the dead squirrel on the mayor's stoop, the Get Well Soon! balloon doorknob-high, then walked home, veering between downed limbs. The enormous typewriter grew louder. It sounded like horses pulling tourists down Savannah's cobblestone streets, microphones hooked to hooves.

He cut through Joe's yard, walked around back, opened his sliding glass door, stepped through, closed it tight, then went to the basement to see if the typewriter followed him. He smelled gas, which was normal, and heard the typewriter still, which was abnormal. In the laundry room, water dripped from the ceiling to the washer (a new development!) directly on top of the graphic novel he and Miles had worked on for six months, Miles with the colored-pencil drawings, both of them on the story about a family being chased by suit-wearing zombies through a burning city. He picked up the soaked pages and held them like a dead pet. Had he carried it to the basement in one hand while he carried dirty clothes in the other, then left the novel on the washer? He looked up to trace the drip, which Maria might call less of a drip and more of a stream.

He put a can beneath the drip, replaced the can with a bucket, then placed the can inside the bucket. Overhead? The kitchen floor. Water came through the same hole a line of copper tubing ran through, and it was streaming alongside the tubing, *outside* the tubing, then falling to the washer. Was last night's windstorm responsible? Should he turn off the water supply? Where was it? Now he had to pee. He went upstairs to the bathroom that faced the street, and looked through the window that faced the driveway, where the fallen tree said *Remember me?* The typist blazed away. While peeing, he worked a math problem: how many minutes does it take to fill a five-gallon bucket at a rate of one drip per second? He couldn't pee long enough to conclude, though he decided that in the minutes it took the bucket to fill, he could clear enough of the tree to move the car. Except. Where had he left his axe? The mayor's stoop?

When he depressed the toilet handle, the city's emergency management siren went off, the painfully loud horn hooked atop the tower planted atop the bluff behind their house. It rotated in a full circle and blared loudly enough to alert every deaf citizen within forty miles. He thought: how did the emergency managers learn about our graphic novel? Then he remembered the siren went off every first Monday of the month at 10 a.m. to let people know what it would sound like when (for example) a train derailed. But it wasn't Monday. Was it? It couldn't yet be 10 a.m., surely. He imagined drowning in an oil spill from a tanker. Burning oil. Oil moving like mud in the mudslide that had killed so many in Sierra Leone. Then he thought: our President, that third grader, has hit the button, making his enemies retaliate. He wondered what God arranged the timing for these things to unravel on *this* day, when he needed to get his son to Rochester? He wondered: what lucky bastard has time for a proper spiritual crisis?

He left the bathroom and stepped outside to see if his wife and child were running in his direction. When the siren swiveled to face him, the typewriter disappeared, and when the siren moved the other way, the typewriter rose again. They *were* coming. They were approaching the bottom of the driveway in no particular hurry while the siren swirled around again and blasted them, forcing Miles to drop Marlin and push his fingers into his ears.

"We have to go," Marty yelled. They couldn't hear him. Already, he was planning their evacuation route, on foot, away from the train, toward higher ground, where he'd summon an Uber or a Lyft to take them all the way to Rochester. Maria stopped in the street, stared at the tree, hands on hips. She pulled her phone from her pocket and texted someone.

"Everything's fine," Marty said. He squatted in front of Miles. The typewriter shrank, and the siren grew, then the siren shrank, and the typewriter grew. The typewriter was taking dictation from the God whose cardinal rule was to honor chaos.

Marty grabbed his son's wrists and pulled his fingers out of his ears. "We'll start a new novel, son. A better one." Miles tried to break free and run inside, but Marty held him, hugged him tight, then Miles's fingers found his ears again. Marty said, "We must have courage." The siren muted the typewriter, then the typewriter appeared again, Max to the front, Dizzy to the rear, Coltrane from the side.

Miles stared toward Mick's roof, so Marty followed his eyes and saw a team of workers up there—eight of them— shooting nail guns into shingles, then the siren stopped and the guns grew louder, firing at the same tempo a fast typist would achieve while hammering out a last will and testament. A camouflaged Jeep pulled up, plastic top zipped tight. A stranger got out and casually approached, a young woman in a Brewers cap. She squatted in front of Miles and winked.

To Marty, the woman said, "I'm driving you to Rochester. I'm Chris."

Marty started crying. Good tears of relief and gratitude that a helper was here.

Maria said, "Zip your pants."

"All aboard," Chris said.

Marty zipped his pants. He climbed in back with Miles, Maria up front. Chris patted Maria's thigh, then squeezed it, as if to say, *everything's fine.* She sped toward the railroad tracks, looked left, then right, left again, then crossed and accelerated.

Marty took Marlin from Miles, raised the fish to his mouth, made the fish say, "Everything's fine."

"Give him back," Miles said.

Chris turned up a Natalie Merchant song Marty had liked long ago. Through the speakers, blending with the bongos, a new typewriter emerged. It started raining, which reminded Marty of the basement leak. How many inches of water would the drip produce in the many hours before they returned? Would the bankers laugh when he said he was underwater? He'd wait to mention this to Maria. No need for another worry on top of the biggest worry of all which they were now speeding toward on this busy road crowded with so many other worried drivers.

"Mom," Miles said. "Dad won't give me Marlin."

Maria released the kind of sigh that came from road-weary carnival workers.

"Marty," Maria said. "Play nice, please."

Chris was an excellent driver, Marty noticed: calm, but assertive enough, flowed with traffic, two car lengths between vehicles, two hands on the wheel, wipers going, headlights on. A single tear hung on each of his cheeks. The typewriter bled between the bongos, playing nice. Marty knew Miles heard it too, based on the way he'd begun to bob his head in sync with his.

Marty held up Marlin, said, "We have a leak in the basement."

"I'll take a look," Chris said. "My mother was a plumber. I learned some things."

Chris touched Maria's leg again, and Maria said something soft that Marty made no effort to understand. He gave Marlin back to Miles, put his arm around his son's shoulder and squeezed. The women started singing.

Marty said, "Hey, Chris—thanks for driving. Thanks for being here. Thank you, Maria, for being here, I love you, and thank you, Miles, for being here, I love you too." Maybe no one heard him over the music, or maybe they preferred the music over him, which was fine because Miles was enjoying himself, still bobbing his head, holding Marlin up now with his other hand, making him flap and dance, flap and dance.

Miles moved Marlin next to his mouth, said, "We're being courageous."

"Your lips were moving," Marty said.

"We're being courageous," said the fish.

"Better," Marty said. "Again, please."

Music Appreciation
for Dead People

When I started this final exam reflection/exit essay (which I wonder if you're even reading) I dialed up the Brahms Alto Rhapsody you played early this semester which you said was so beautiful it made some suicidal writer change his mind, so I gave it another chance thinking I'd missed something, and guess what? It still sucks. So I changed it up and started listening to what my twin brother was playing when I found him, which I'm not even going to tell you what it was. You wouldn't appreciate it. You'd probably have a spasm like you did that day when somebody asked what you thought of Lil Nas X, who, you know what? was at least trying some new things unlike some professors who repeat the same boring-ass lecture for forty years, keeping to the script from two thousand years ago when the killer B's as you called them (Brahms, Beethoven, and Bach—to which I would add Bon Iver) were making the crowds go wild. This is my final final exam/reflection/ exit essay ever because after much reflection I've decided to exit this college, which is a decision you helped me make. I appreciate it.

What you really want to hear is how everything you played really opened our eyes, but the truth is I didn't appreciate anything about your mix. Music without a drumbeat is impossible to tap your foot to. Maybe I missed something during those two weeks I was out, but I doubt it, not that you noticed my absence. Not that you even replied to my email where I said I'd be absent, which would have been nice, just to have that little bit of human interaction, but maybe you never reply to anyone's email, which is par for the course here at this prestigious state institution. Ha. Par for the course. Good one, Rylie. Thanks.

I was out two weeks because I got Covid on purpose so I could sell my plasma. My Dad's idea. He said if I got it, I could make a lot more from the plasma. Which is funny because when I was a kid, he called me "Hypo," short for hypochondriac, because I was constantly worried about germs and also whether I'd get diabetes from having a sip of Diet Coke. And I figured if I got Covid, at least I'd have a good excuse for some excused absences.

The sad part is that I had a hard time getting it because I couldn't get close enough to anyone. I never met people who knew people who threw parties. I'm not good at talking, and if I ever get out of my comfort zone to even try to talk to someone new, like a friend beside me, like my roommate, but he lasted three weeks before he went home. My twin brother and I were supposed to be roommates, but then I got stuck with this guy who was the filthiest person on the planet, he never cared about reducing his body odor or helping with cleanliness, so I'm the one who vacuumed, swiffered, and wiped down everything while he played Mortal Kombat and listened to screamo metal, his favorite album being "You Can't Spell Slaughter Without Laughter" by a band called I Set My Friends on Fire. My favorite track is "Reese's Pieces, I don't know who John Cleese is?" which is upbeat, and it doesn't matter that I also don't know who John Cleese is.

His other favorite band was I Killed the Prom Queen, in particular the song, "Sharks in your mouth" on the album "Music for the Recently Deceased (tour edition")), which you would run rapidly away from if you were accidentally exposed to it is my guess. He said it got him through his days though, which I appreciated. Then he got Covid and went home and I missed him. Remember when you said nobody listens to albums anymore? My ex-roommate listened to albums and my brother was listening to an album in his car when I found him, an actual CD because the old car my dad got for him had a CD player in it, which you can't find anymore. I'm not even going to mention what album it was.

That day you devoted to the 1960s when you played Jimmy Hendricks doing his Star-Spangled Banner thing was okay, but then you saw some people covering their ears and some-body asked what drugs he was on and you said maybe the problem was that *we* weren't doing enough drugs. Which is where I think you could do some reflecting yourself and see whether you want to say things like that or not because that's how my brother died, an overdose. My parents want to believe it was an accident, but I knew him better and saw it coming. He hated school more than anyone in history, and here he was about to go college, which he hated the thought of, but he didn't want to stay home either, and then his girlfriend broke up with him and started trashing him on Snapchat, and then he got kicked out of the band he'd been playing drums with which he took really hard because that's all he wanted to do forever was to be a rocknroll drummer. Maybe he wasn't good enough at that point or maybe the other guys didn't like him much, I don't know, he never said.

So I had a hard time getting Covid, but Dad said, "be persistent." I sat closer to people in the cafeteria, and bingo, fevers and chills for a couple days, then I was pretty sure I was going to die (even though my mom promised I wouldn't), and then I recovered and started selling plasma and made

$400 after just two donations which wasn't enough to pay for college and I knew Dad was taking out extra loans, which was a lot of money to pay for me to be miserable, so I started thinking I should drop out and help Dad, which would help Mom too because she was exhausted and she'd been crying nonstop, but I didn't want to go back to our tiny town either.

One of the things that killed my brother off was how Dad lost his right hand in a piece of farm machinery, which was my brother's fault. He didn't lock the combine header when Dad crawled underneath it to pull out a rock. It was almost dark and Dad couldn't see the blades were still spinning, and Aaron never heard him, or he was daydreaming, I don't know. I picked up his hand and ran to the house and Mom dropped it in a bucket of ice and drove us all to the hospital, which is a period of time I wouldn't mind forgetting. Dad took it surprisingly well, considering, but then another thing that killed Aaron off was how Dad went around the farm saying "Lend me a hand." It was funny the first time. But not the next ten thousand times. Aaron wanted to forget about it too and move far away but he fell in love with drugs instead is my theory.

When I got to campus the first day, I felt like a sign was stuck to my face saying "Hick Alert" and I know some of that was my own imagination turning against me, but not all of it. I started to believe I smelled like cow shit. Our town is so small it's not even a town, it's a village. I didn't meet anyone else who came from such a small place or whose parents had never gone to college and hearing my roommate who was from Milwaukee talk to his friends made me feel more alone. Even my freshman comp teacher made me feel bad after I wrote an essay about the stereotypes I was hearing about farm kids and how I was "tired of being pigeon-toed," which is where she put a laughing emoji in the margin. Here's a confession: you know when you *required* us to attend the symphony? I didn't go. Maybe if you had bought my ticket and also bought me some new clothes and a car I would've gone, but probably not.

Drake. That's what he was listening to. I don't know why I was scared to mention it. It's not like you've even made it this far and it's not like you've even heard of Drake. I won't bother telling you what album it was.

I'm surprised I made it to the end of this first semester because I wanted to leave the moment my folks dropped me off. You know what was playing during move-in day? Whoever's in charge of that mix needs to get fired asap. Because Journey? "Separate Ways?" Followed by "Who's Crying Now?" While all the parents are losing their shit and the kids are about to be abandoned? Unless they were trying to be funny. But no one was laughing, and it felt like it was going out to all the grandparents in the crowd so they could recognize something from the previous century that would make them feel like everything was going to be okay.

So there's Dad, blubbering away, wiping his nose with his stub, standing next to his truck with the door open after we'd made three trips up three flights of dorm stairs, though we got some help from volunteers wearing smiley-face shirts, and after the last trip, my dad said, I guess that's it, which is more than he'd said over the previous three hours we'd been riding in his truck listening to his favorite CD of all time—his only CD, come to think of it—Hank Williams Sr.'s greatest hits, which, I have to admit, kind of grew on me. Hank had women troubles, money troubles, homesick troubles. His bucket had a hole in it. I looked up some other songs he did as Luke the Drifter, which I made the mistake of sampling for my roommate, which he failed to appreciate. He laughed and started talking in a ridiculous southern accent, then made a big show of putting on his noise-canceling headphones so the screaming could be closer to his brain.

After I hugged Mom and Dad goodbye, I reached into the truck and hugged my dog, which was the hardest thing. He'd made the trip with us, of course—Hank, we'd named him, after Williams, because that's who Dad was playing that Christmas morning ten years ago when he brought in this puppy through the back door who ran toward us and jumped all over us but also after Hank Aaron because my brother's name was Aaron and because Dad told us how Hank Aaron played in Milwaukee before going to Atlanta and broke Babe Ruth's all-time homerun record. Hank was supposed to be for both of us, but he stuck to Aaron from the get-go. Afterward, he slept with me. He raised his head every time he heard a noise like Aaron might be coming home, so I felt extra lonely when he went back home without me.

That Drake album is called *If You're Reading This It's Too Late*. There was one song on there called "Used To," featuring Lil Wayne, which I never want to hear again. He'd driven his car to the far side of the corn field next to our pond (this was early August when the corn was head-high) and I found him there on a Sunday morning after my mom had made a big breakfast for us, pancakes and maple syrup, and when he didn't come down, I went out and walked around and found him. A month later, they dropped me off, and Mom was blubbering (she never really stopped) because she was going to be on her own with Dad, keeping the books and seeing about the loans and doing work she didn't want to do, and all I could think at the time was I couldn't wait for them to leave, but when they left, I wanted them to come back.

If there was one day of class that helped the most with my decision to drop out it was that day you devoted to funeral music. Next semester, in addition to the useless textbook you required us to buy for fifty bucks, I'd recommend you pass around some anti-depressants so everyone can supplement their supply. And you should retitle the course "Music Appreciation for Dead People."

A week after my roommate left, someone started peeing outside my dorm room door. There was a nice little puddle in the hall I had to step over every time I went out. Maybe more than one person, I don't know. Maybe word got out that I was a country-music-loving neat-freak everyone decided they should hate. So I spent more time in the library, camped out in a dark corner cubicle up on the sixth floor with my earbuds in and one night I saw this couple having sex up there which was depressing. They didn't know I was there, I guess, or maybe they did and were doing it for my benefit so they could show me up close what I was missing out on during my college experience, and I was listening to Bon Iver's album "For Emma, Forever Ago", and about the time that couple started going at it is when "Skinny Love" came on, which now I can't even listen to without thinking about that specific night in the library or that specific time in my life when Bon Iver kept me company. Justin Vernon, the singer, wrote that whole album while he secluded himself in his father's hunting cabin which is about an hour from where I grew up, and he sings like he's also having severe isolation, so that's an album I appreciate.

One thing I got homesick for was my Dad's terrible mac and cheese. He always put sliced up hot dogs in it, which I never appreciated at the time. I don't mind the natural casing hot dogs that give you a little crunch, but the pre-cooked squishy Oscar Mayer wieners were not my meat of choice. Why contaminate perfectly good mac and cheese with an overly processed tube of meat filled with miscellaneous animal parts? But then its funny what you start missing.

> I ain't felt the pressure in a little while
> It's gon' take some getting used to
> Floatin' all through the city with the windows down
> Puttin' on like I used to

They never told me when you get the crown
It's gon' take some getting used to
New friends all in their old feelings now
They don't love you like they used to man.

(Drake ft Wayne, Lil)

Dad made Aaron keep his drums in the hay barn, which is where he played every day after school (after chores) and then again after dinner for hours in the dark until Mom sent me out there to make him stop so we could go to bed, and it was around this time, in May of our senior year, when school was almost out, that he got more depressed and wouldn't talk to me or anyone else, and no one knew what to do or what to say without him erupting like a lunatic, and we were all kind of afraid of him by then, and we thought, well, as long as we hear the drums coming from the hay barn, maybe he's okay, and that summer they let him play out there all night in the dark if he wanted to, and by then, it was pretty amazing what he was doing—like he had eight arms and eight legs. He ran an extension cord out there and plugged in a stereo and started playing along with Bonham and Peart and Moon, but then he also played along with some jazz drummers like Art Blakey and Max Roach, which is when I thought, wow, my brother is strange. But if you could've heard him out there—could've heard what was coming out of that barn through the darkness, you would have stopped in your tracks to appreciate it. You would have wondered where does Bonham stop and my brother begin?

Remember that day in class you got way off the subject and started talking about the President and how dumb he was for cutting the arts, which I can actually agree with, especially because of my brother, who I would say was an artist. But that was the same day you gave us the history of music influenced by drugs and maybe you were having a bad day based on how you went off on us for hating the Beatles and Hendricks and you said we should be doing more drugs, well, that struck a nerve at the time based on my brother's experience so if your wondering who slid that angry note under your office door, guess who? Which reminds me: The Guess Who. That one song you played from that band was okay: "Lonely feeling, deep inside, find a corner, where I can hide. Silent footsteps crowding me. Sudden darkness, but I can see." And no sugar in their coffee or tea? I also don't like sugar, so I appreciated that song.

If you ever met my brother, the first thing you would notice is that he's a douche bag. The second thing you'd notice is that there's a big room behind his eyes full of nooks and crannies where a special kind of music is playing that's like it was made for only him which made it hard for him to hear anyone else. Then it's like his music got louder after the accident. Because an awkward situation everybody wants to avoid is to have a hand cut off inside a piece of farm machinery, especially if it's your own son's fault. Dad tried to make the best of it, tried to shoot left-handed, but that put more pressure on me and Aaron to kill a deer we could put in the freezer. We both wanted no part of our annual deer-hunting trips which Aaron made sure he was super-high for. High on hunting, he called it. I didn't like hunting either. If I ever got a shot off, I made sure to miss. Aaron missed on purpose too and Dad cussed at us, said we'd have to go hungry, but we knew there was always a surplus of mac and cheese with cut up hotdogs. At the end of the first day of deer season, everybody meets in the only bar in town where the walls are over-populated with deer heads staring at you. Dad bought us beers which is legal if your a minor whose guardian is buying it for you (in case you don't know about the state laws, based on your accent I'm guessing your not from around here), but I never liked the taste of beer. I didn't like the gossip I heard there either. This one guy was always making fun of the Amish on the outskirts of town and he'd spread rumors about how they had sexual relations with their animals and he'd make it sound like you should feel sorry for the animals, but then I'd feel ashamed of myself for imagining such acts. These stories made me want to get away from there and go to college where I thought people wouldn't spend so much time talking about other people, but I was wrong about that. I even had this one professor who liked to talk about his co-workers. It's like he got bullied as a kid and had to return the favor for the rest of his life, which I don't care how fat he is, but it showed me that even the most educated are no different than the least educated in their gossiping ways, and it was like I'm paying for *this*?

Mom would meet us at the bar, and she'd be drinking and trying to have fun too, and sometimes instead of making fun of me for not liking the beer Dad ordered for me, she'd wait until he wasn't looking and drink it for me. There was a juke-box in there where people played the kind of country music I didn't appreciate, but Mom played some classics I liked, her favorite being John Conley's "Rose Colored Glasses" which made her sad, but she sang along with it too, which made her happy, along with it being around beer number three that put a certain look in her eyes like she wouldn't mind having a different life. But there was something about his voice that got me too, something in there that felt more real than the other voices. You'd probably go off on a snob-filled lecture on what was wrong with it, but that song will always make me think of those moments in the bar with my mom, who deserves some happiness.

If I'd had a date, I might've gone to the symphony. I never had a girlfriend and didn't see any way I would ever get one. Being able to speak properly is a big quality to have in order to make someone fall in love with you. Some people can keep the conversation going by giving weird facts or asking questions. My brother was good at conversations so there aren't those awkward silences, which is how he fooled us into thinking he was okay while he was really just fooling my parents into giving him drug money. But I never know what to say, and every single day in every class while people wait for the professors like you to start going blah, blah, blah, everyone's looking at their phones and texting other people and never saying anything at all to the person who's sitting right next to them and sometimes I would text my dead brother just to fit in. Some days I think I saw a look on your face like you could relate, but then class would start and that face got replaced with professor-face, which meant get ready to be bored.

Being alone too long is bad for the brain. Some people are shy, so if you as a professor make someone feel bad after calling on them and asking them to say something and they never do, well, maybe that person needs more time to understand the question or maybe in addition to trying to stay awake they're working a full-time job (which I'm guessing is something you didn't have to do in college) and at that moment their brain is not available and they've already done a miraculous job of just getting out of bed and marching across campus in zero-degree weather while thinking about their dead brother and then they climb three flights of stairs to sit in a room around people staring at their phones and when they still don't know what to say after the long pause you provide to enhance the embarrassment, you take it personally and enact some retribution along the lines of failing them when maybe you should reflect a little harder on how to say hello out there (and learn an actual name or two), are you okay?

Because maybe we're not. Maybe we have things on our mind that you didn't have on your mind when you were our age. When I was in church one Sunday in eighth grade the priest decided to ask us what nightmares we'd been having lately and a four-year-old girl raised her hand and said "someone comes into church and kills us." The whole congregation got silent. It's like that kid's childhood was dead at that point, and I think she killed mine too because that was the day I lost my faith. I don't even remember what I was doing at the age of four, but it was most definitely not worrying about a church shooter. One nightmare I have is living at home for the rest of my life and coming home from a job I hate and seeing Mom in the kitchen where instead of saying "how was school" she says "how was work?" and me having even less to say.

I'm not a very social person, only having one close friend from home, Billy Preston, who I hardly talk to anymore because he says I've changed, which I guess is true, so I think he's now a former friend which means I'm down to no friends. This semester, I've tried sticking my neck out in the realm of romance, and every time I get a feeling I might have found someone, I disappoint myself. I try to figure out what I do wrong, which leaves me feeling empty. There was never a day that passed over my entire first semester when I felt like, hey, I belong here, it's such a cool place for people like me who have no fucking clue what they want to do and no interest in studying or going to a class to listen to some stale lecture or some terrible music I'm required to appreciate. Some say all first-year students are on the same boat, but it doesn't feel like it.

I have yet to see a final exam that measures the size of a human heart. Maybe Brahms had a brother who died on him, maybe he put his broken heart into his piano and said let's see what comes out the other side that someone else might find some comfort in, I don't know, but if it works for you, that's great. People have different ways of dealing: screaming, coloring, running, taking drugs, drinking, listening to music, playing music. Writing? I've never thought about that one because I never thought I had much to say or that anyone would even want to listen, but I've been rambling here for awhile because it's making me feel less depressed. So all in all, this is me expressing my appreciation to you for giving me my best failure ever. I hope you're able to reflect upon your own failures and imagine a better future for yourself.

Somehow, I picture you doing just that while all the dead musicians you exposed us to gather around your bed or couch or swimming pool, which makes me feel slightly better for some strange reason, like you could use their company. I hope they help you. Good luck. I'm going to the barn now. I'm going to take a notebook out there and I'm going to lay it on top of my brother's snare drum, and then I'm going to write something just for him that I know he would appreciate.

What Unites Us

Joseph thought he deserved a medal for not kicking his boss's ass, the twenty-two-year-old pissant son of the company's owner, who was scolding him now at quitting time, Friday, with the sun bearing down as hard as it had all day every day of the endless summer. He imagined Melissa, his pregnant girlfriend, pinning the medal to his chest, congratulating him on remaining calm. The pissant squinted, about to break a sweat for the first time in his life, which threatened to dislodge his perfect hair.

Joseph, twice the kid's age, listened to the kid explain the horror of being behind schedule with so many retaining walls having

Joe's last patient canceled, saying they wanted a kind physician capable of listening, so he went home early, dismissed the babysitter and told his two sons to put on their gear because *today*—a hot Friday afternoon—was the day they would bike down Bliss.

"But Mom said never do that," said Scottie, his five-year-old.

"Stop being a pussy," said Aidan, his nine-year-old.

"Don't call your brother a pussy," said Joe, the forty year-old.

He loaded their bikes and drove them to the top of the bluff so they could launch themselves from the highest

162

collapsed from the previous week's record-breaking rain. Joe wondered: did the kid get a *weekly* haircut? The pissant was telling him he did *not* need to put the level on top of every single block he set in place, a point Joseph disagreed with as a craftsman who took pride in building perfectly symmetrical walls. *This* $20,000 wall was meant to protect a half-million-dollar home, tricky with its forty-five degree angles and varying heights.

Joseph looked into the kid's eyes, a five and a quarter-inch drop. He thought: wouldn't Ma be proud if she saw the peaceful man he'd become? She had tried so hard to make him a gentleman, to say he shouldn't be like his father, whose influence proved stronger, even from prison, where he was serving time for *retaliating* to an asshole. Joseph was staying sober, working steady, eager to be a better father than his father had been, saving for the day he and Melissa could leave their crappy duplex and

point, 703 feet, Scottie in the tagalong attached to Joe's bike, Aidan—already a skilled biker—to coast down on his right. He squatted in front of them, tightened their helmets, tapped his knuckles on their heads. Mei, his wife, needed to know she shouldn't be so anxious. She had promised to divorce him and take custody of the boys should Joe take it upon himself to take such risks, but he knew they were ready. She'd grown up in Beijing (pop. 30 million, give/take) and claimed it was safer to bike there than here (pop. 50,000), where drivers raced to cover short distances. Joe had twice been knocked off his bike, received regular middle-fingers and horn blows. Last year, two college students were killed in a crosswalk, which Joe argued was even more reason to teach his boys courage *and* safety. He commuted daily by bike, changed tires in winter, wore bright clothes, goggles, flashing lights on his helmet *and* the upstairs drug dealer to a tree-filled neighborhood with kind neighbors.

Joseph counted to ten while the pissant told him to return to the site the next day, Saturday, after which, he should think hard about whether he wanted to return Monday as a team player because there were lots of go-getters working shovels who would love to be promoted to wall-builder.

Joseph's dad's voice said, *How much shit are you going to take from this pissant?*

Joseph told his eyes to inform the pissant that his little power trip was amusing. He told his eyes to inform him that he should learn to relax before a heart attack killed him.

Melissa's voice said, *Come home now.*

Joseph's throbbing lower back said, *We could use some relief down here.* His dry throat said, *Wouldn't twelve cold beers be a paradise worth revisiting?*

The kid's eyes were telling Joseph that he had squandered his life. His Ma said, *Go home to Melissa.* Joseph

belt, supplied hand signals he'd already taught the boys.

They coasted carefully now, Aidan to his right, Joe padding his brakes so they'd match pace. Solo, he *never* touched his brakes, maxing out near fifty mph down the final stretch according to the odometer he got last year when they bought the overpriced house on the bluff, then added debt with solar panels, new appliances. Now, a new bill of $20,000 for a retaining wall to replace the wall that collapsed last week from record-breaking rains, which meant more money was needed to fix the flooded basement, *an unfortunate act of God,* the insurance agent said.

On weekends, he biked a hundred miles to out-pedal money worries, his wife's grief, whose parents died in China a year ago, his own mom with ALS, his dad, dead from Covid, his brother, an anti-vaxxer. He biked so he could sleep, but often woke at 2 a.m. to read reviews from patients who walked away. In his head, he said, *look Ma, I'm walking away.*

He got into his truck, which was his father's truck, busted muffler and all. He squeezed the wheel and sped down Bliss Road, passing a biker and his two kids, all of them in shiny expensive-looking spandex, taking up the entire lane, forcing Joseph to accelerate to get around them so he wouldn't cream the oncoming Subaru. He thought: what kind of shitty father takes his kids down a steep road with no bike lane at rush hour?

When the red light caught him at the bottom, he loosened his grip on the wheel and looked across four lanes of traffic as if he could see into Melissa's eyes. He texted *otw.* She'd be getting antsy now, being locked inside the duplex all day, which *she* had insisted on. She didn't trust herself to go all day without visiting the upstairs dealer.

She texted a gif of a cheerleader.

Next thing he knew, someone with fancy complained of his *arrogance* and blunt *demeanor.*

They coasted down the final stretch when the truck sped by, nearly grazing Joe's left elbow, a blatant violation of state statute 346.48(1), stipulating vehicles allow three feet of space to bikers. Then a gunshot from the muffler which made Scottie scream, then diesel fumes that felt like drowning in tar, then the bumper sticker supporting the idiot who declared the epidemic a hoax and named it the kung-fu virus, fueling racist fervor Mei had heard too often.

At the red light, Joe sped to the sidewalk, yelled at his boys to stay *exactly* where they were and jogged his bike toward the truck's passenger side window, eager to educate an asshole. He wanted to teach his boys that one could engage bullies in conversations that lead to transformational moments whereby bullies come to understand the value of community over selfishness.

He tapped on the guy's window and recited

sunglasses was banging on his passenger side window—the biker he'd passed a minute earlier. Dude was pissed. Over his shoulder, the biker's kids stood on the sidewalk, watching, mouths hanging open.

Joseph flipped him off. He looked at the light, still red. The guy kept yelling things Joseph couldn't hear over his busted muffler.

Then the asshole did something stupid. He walked his bike, which had a small bike attached to the back of it, (a very expensive-looking shiny combo) in front of Joseph's truck and laid it on the ground, stood behind it and raised his left palm like a traffic cop. Joseph thought: what kind of bad father teaches such shit to kids? He thought: would the poor kids remember this as a pivotal moment as they grew into entitled brats?

The lunatic looked like he wanted to pull Joseph out of his truck and strangle him. The light turned green. Did he have any choice but to run over the guy's state statute 346.48(1) on behalf of his boys and the eighty-member Bike Brigade for which he served as Treasurer, a group of good citizens who championed bikers' rights and zero emissions.

The asshole flipped him off. Here was a neanderthal who found music in loud trucks, who would bottle diesel fumes into cologne.

He walked his $8,000 bike around to the front of the truck, lay it gently in the street to stall the driver so he could go to his window and recite the statute. He raised his palm as a stop sign, then approached the driver's window and asked him whether he'd consider sharing the fucking road more respectfully, if not for him, then for the safety of his two children and for all the bikers who were, per statute 346.48(1) entitled to three feet.

The fool hit the gas and ran right over his right foot. Then his bicycle. Then kept going. Joe sat in the middle of the street, face full of bike? What was wrong with people?

He passed three convenience stores full of beer. And kept going. They'd been clean and sober six months, since learning Melissa was pregnant. He imagined telling her this story, how he'd avoided trouble with his boss, then avoided trouble with the biker. He imagined them taking an evening walk to the river, then later asking whether she felt like applying her magical massage-skills on his aching back. Over the weekend they'd planned to look at a list of houses Melissa made, all of them out of their price range, but the act of looking gave them something to dream toward.

They'd been saving less lately because of what they'd given doctors, trying to learn why Melissa couldn't stay on her feet long enough to work at the salon, where they'd started giving away her shifts. They waited for test results that might lead to other tests. She worried her stress was hurting the baby, that it would come

diesel fumes, memorized the license plate, called 911 to report an aggravated assault.

People stopped to ask if he was okay, to help him to the sidewalk, to carry his squashed bicycle to the curb. One witness said he should file manslaughter charges, and another expressed urgent hope that the truck driver would be severely punished.

He hoped Mei would listen long enough to hear him say it wasn't his fault, that he was merely promoting safety. They had planned a weekend trip to their cabin up north, and once they all got into the canoe and paddled across the lake at sunset, they'd all be fine again.

Later, when he replayed the moment, he remembered Tank Man, the dissident who blocked the path of a tank during the anti-war uprising in Tiananmen Square, 1989. He made a note then to show the boys the famous YouTube clip, to say, "See? That's what courage looks like." But he knew out missing a leg or a kidney.

When he pulled in front of the duplex, two cop cars were already there. Melissa had the curtain pulled back, looking out, one hand on her stomach, eyes full of heartbreak. Joseph got out of his truck and shook his head toward her, telling her it was nothing. Two cops came from one side, one from the other.

One cop said, "We have a report claiming you ran over a biker?"

"No," Joe said. "That fucker—"

"Looky here," said a fourth cop, returning from Joseph's truck, holding up a pill bottle. His bottle of Oxy from the upstairs neighbor.

Joseph looked at Melissa, who saw the cop hold up the bottle. She watched another cop pull Joseph's hands behind his back and cuff him. Her eyes said *how could you fuck up now, you lying stupid fuck.*

Joseph said, "Can I unlock the door for my girlfriend? She's locked inside. She's—"

Mei would say, "So? Where is Tank Man now? Dead from execution? In prison?" And between them in that moment would be the *thing*—that incident from a year ago when Joe lost his temper when he stopped the Tesla (Mei's) at a red light and a truck tapped his rear bumper, where his own bumper stickers resided— clearly an act of aggression. Joe responded by jumping out of the car (with Mei in the passenger seat and the boys in the back) and yelled at the truck driver who asked Joe to please come closer so he could punch him in his mouth. Then the light changed and horns honked and Joe pulled his phone out and snapped a pic of the driver he took to the police station, where a cop laughed at the subject's raised middle finger.

Later that night in their bedroom, Mei informed Joe that the very next time he decided to behave in a similar manner that put himself and his children in danger, she would leave

"That's funny," a cop said. "Because *you're* about to be locked inside."

Joseph's eyes tried to tell her not to worry. He was telling her the Oxy was for his back, that he took one every morning before he started lifting blocks, another at day's end.

"Can I just tell her what's happening?"

"You can call her in a minute," a cop said.

She closed the curtain.

He called her an hour later, said, "Listen. Everything's fine. This guy—"

"What did you do?"

"Listen."

"I can't believe you." She was crying.

"Listen. This biker was going down Bliss Road with his two kids, and—"

"You hit a biker? And his kids?"

"No, listen. He—"

"I'm going to give birth while you're in jail, you selfish fucker. I'm not—"

"Listen, goddamnit. He—"

"I knew you couldn't stay clean."

him instantly and take the boys, then turned off her light. An hour later, he said, "You're right," but she was softly snoring. He thought of his mother, who had tried to raise him to be a gentleman, how ashamed she'd be. He thought of his librarian father, who had never once raised his voice. He thought of a patient review that called him arrogant.

He couldn't put much weight on his right foot, but otherwise, yes, he was fine.

A cop collected his statement, and statements of witnesses. He stood on one leg and turned to his boys, asking if they were okay. They all still had their helmets on, straps fastened, staring at the ground.

"This wasn't our fault," Joe told them. "And that's what we're telling your mother."

He called her. She'd be commuting home now after spending another long day as a hospital administrator dealing with personnel who dealt all day with the endless exhaustion that came from dealing with staffing

Joe saw the biker's face now and wanted very badly to beat him to death.

"Listen," he said. "I'm not on probation anymore. I'll bond out. I'll call my boss and he'll bail me out and I'll be home, and—"

"I won't be here. I'm not staying here alone while you're in jail."

"You can't leave. The door's locked."

"I've already been out. Kitchen window, dummy. Guess where I went?" She hung up.

They gave him a second call to arrange bond. He called the pissant's father, Bruce, who'd hired him after doing a background check, saying he believed in second chances. Bruce said he'd send his son.

The pissant picked him up and drove him home. He pointed to his glovebox, said he would've done worse, said he'd recently pointed his gun at a slow-driving fool in the fast lane of the interstate. Then the pissant said, like he should be applauded, that they'd keep Joseph's next check for repayment.

shortages that made it so difficult to deal with the endless stream of unvaccinated patients who kept demanding life-saving attention.

"We're okay," he told her right away. "We're fine. This—"

"What're you talking about?"

"This asshole in a truck just ran over my bike *and* my foot at the bottom of Bliss. I think he broke a navicular bone. I can barely stand on it, but the boys were on the sidewalk, and they're fine."

"They boys were with you?"

"They're fine."

"I see you." She hung up.

Joe looked across the intersection, saw her car, first in line at the opposite light, facing him. She pulled up beside him, got out quickly, squatted in front of both boys, examined their faces and got them in the car.

While Joe stepped gingerly from the sidewalk, Mei closed her door and zoomed off. He stood beside

By the time he got home, soft light fell on the neighborhood, people filled porches, someone was grilling. Down the sidewalk, his blind neighbor, Lewis, carried home his daily twelve pack, and racing toward him now was a kid on a tricycle wearing a diaper and no shirt, pedaling like a demon, elbows raised.

He turned the deadbolt, stepped into the duplex, so quiet now it scared him. The kitchen window was open. He called her phone. No answer.

Joseph stormed upstairs, knocked on Reggie's door, identified himself, knocked again until Reggie opened up, wearing a bathrobe and slippers, eyes barely open.

Reggie said, "Why you wanna bring 5-0 'round? What kinda shit you done been into?"

"What did you give Melissa?"

"That's doctor-patient confidential, man."

Joseph pinned Reggie against the wall, said, "I'll break your fucking neck."

his crumpled bike, hands on hips, watched her leave. Here was the test he'd failed when she'd said "don't test me."

He hoisted his squashed bike, tagalong still attached, over his left shoulder, lifted Aidan's bike in his right hand and limped up Bliss. Traffic veered around him, sometimes stopping to avoid oncoming cars, drivers' faces looking tortured because of the extra seconds this required. He limped on, hung his head, imagined himself as Sisyphus. He moved sideways, crab-like, because it hurt less that way. Did Sisyphus have a wife whose eternal punishment was to forever watch him do the same dumb thing? Was it as hot where he was as it was here, where another record-breaking day near one hundred degrees turned people crazy? Or did the wife of Sisyphus say, after his second trip, I refuse to keep watching this?

An hour later, he dropped the bikes in his driveway. The garage door was open, the

"You need a Oxy refill, ain't it?" Reggie said. "On the house."

Joseph let him go, followed Reggie to his kitchen. "She said something about a bus to Florida. Said you was 'bout to get sent up. What you do?"

Her mother lived in Florida, was recovering from lung cancer. Joseph had talked to her on the phone several times, promised he'd take care of her little girl, promised they'd come for a visit soon.

Reggie handed him a bottle Joseph took downstairs. He called Melissa again. No answer. He kept calling, kept telling the story in little chunks for as long as he could until it cut him off, then called back and resumed, explained how the biker had asked for it, how the pissant had been riding his ass, how all he wanted was for her to be home.

In the morning, he called again, left a message saying he was going to work, that he was working to save for their new house.

garage empty. He entered the house, called "Hello?" Heard nothing. In the kitchen, he looked for a note. Nothing. In the top cabinet behind a collection of spices, he reached for a bottle that held a few Hydrocodone he took on rare weekends when he rode so long it rendered his back and butt too sore to sleep. He pulled a pack of frozen peas from the freezer and limped to the couch, raised his swollen foot on one end, put the peas on top. He checked his phone. No messages. He called Mei. No answer. Left a message.

"You need to hear the whole story. Let me explain. I made sure the boys were safe. I'm sorry you don't trust me. I mean, I'm sorry I give you reason to worry. I hear that."

Had she taken the boys to the cabin? Was she talking to a lawyer? The big house went deeply quiet. The quiet house went dark, said, *How do you like me now?* He texted, *let's talk pls.* The dark house said, *You really are arrogant.* She didn't text

After an hour, he took a smoke break, squatted on a block, felt the pinch in his lower back. He looked through the woods, imagining Melissa's face if she could see these orioles taking turns at a cup of jelly the homeowner had hung between two orange halves, how she'd giggle at the chipmunks racing around with fat cheeks. Earlier, a doe and her fawn strolled by, so close it looked like they wanted to eat out of his hand. He stared deeply into the mother's eyes, told her he wasn't about to hurt her beautiful baby, then gingerly pulled his phone out and took a picture, thinking he'd send it to Melissa, who would say, "Can we live there, please?"

Behind him, a sliding glass door opened and clumsy footsteps came across the back porch. He dropped his cigarette beside his boot and mashed it out, picked up the butt and dropped it in his shirt pocket.

"Hey," the man said. "No smoking."

Joseph raised his hands to show they were empty, back. He texted, *ok, let's sleep on it. Tomorrow will be better.*

He woke on the sunroom couch, light slanting in, pack of peas on the floor, foot the size of a cantaloupe, throbbing, the house too quiet. Through the tall windows, he saw the retaining wall worker sitting on a block, facing the woods, smoking. He checked his phone, no messages. He called Mei, no answer. *I'm sorry,* he texted. *Point taken. I'm an asshole. I'll go to therapy again. Come home pls. Second chance, pls.*

He smelled the worker's cigarette and thought of Mei, whose father died from lung cancer. She could smell a cigarette from three miles, would grimace, flap a hand in front of her nose and curse, louder if the smoker was in a space her children shared. The guy sat there, smoking, staring into the woods. Joe lifted himself gingerly from the couch and hopped to the sliding glass door, eager to educate an asshole.

"Hey," he said. "No smoking."

then turned, saw the spandex outfit, the guy holding up his swollen foot while he descended the steps holding both rails. Here was the man who had banged on his father's truck, who yelled and cursed, who lay his bike in front of his tires, invited him to run over it and *then* called the cops. His hair was wild, eyes glazed, and his foot, swollen and purple, hung limply off the ground.

The guy kept coming, one hand on the wall. What one-legged short fool hopped toward a big man with a look in his eye like he was bent on murder? He remembered Melissa looking through the window while the cops cuffed him, an hour in a jail cell crowded with dealers trading stories, how he repeated his own story to people who swore he was in the right, how he worried over a judge who would take his one and only prior from ten years ago too seriously, the open kitchen window, the $1,000 dollars he now owed the pissant, the weekend he and Melissa would not spend looking at houses,

He descended the steps by using both rails as crutches, left foot aloft. When he reached the bottom he looked up, saw the face he'd seen yesterday, saw the age and exhaustion there, saw how he stooped a little, his bushy beard and American flag bandana wrapped around his head. *This* guy, who had run over his foot and his $8,000 bike and had maybe caused his divorce. Joe kept one hand on the wall, hopped closer.

What he saw in the guy's eyes reminded him of his dumbass brother, prideful and primitive, resentful of bosses, educated by Fox News. But they'd hugged at their father's funeral. Their mother told them to try harder, and they talked then of bringing their families together at the cabin.

The big guy stood there like a deaf and mute Neanderthal. Joe didn't want to think of this guy every time he saw his retaining wall. He didn't want to remember Scottie screaming when the prick's truck went by, or see the guy flipping him off, how he ran over her eyes going to the bottle of Oxy the cop held, then back to his eyes, the closed curtain, the empty duplex, the inside of the dark and smelly bus Melissa rode all night to Florida.

For a second, Joseph imagined a scenario where he'd give him a ride to the hospital, which might prompt the prick to apologize, to drop the charges, then he'd offer his own apology. He imagined telling *that* story to Melissa *and* her mother, a happy ending.

"Get off my property," he said.

Joseph thought: *I should walk away.* The guy kept coming. An arrogant and entitled rich prick so used to making demands, getting what he wanted. The guy pointed to the road and made an expression like a drooling idiot, speaking slowly, mocking Joseph.

"Leave my property," the prick said.

He pushed Joseph. Joseph pushed back, knocked him down, and in the same fluid motion, lifted the block he'd been sitting on and raised it

his bicycle as if he enjoyed it, how Mei scooped the boys away, how he limped up the bluff with a broken foot, how Mei maybe wasn't coming back. He certainly didn't want to give money to someone whose belief system (according to his bumper sticker) aligned with a hate-filled tyrant. He'd finish the wall himself if he had to. That way, he could trick his mind into believing he'd built the whole thing. He'd look at it with a sense of pride for taking a stand.

"Get off of my property."

What kind of Neanderthal just stands there like a deaf statue when he's being asked by a homeowner to get off his property? There was something in his eyes like he wasn't home and never would be. Joe pointed toward the front of the house.

"Leave my property," Joe said.

Joe put one finger on his chest and nudged him, a simple sign that he should back up and keep going. The guy swatted his hand and thrust his open palm into Joe's chest so hard it above his head. His father said *kill that motherfucker.*

His mother said *walk away, Joseph.*

Melissa said, *will you ever see your child?*

His father's voice was winning. Then Melissa's eyes appeared as they had the day before from behind the window, looking so hurt it made him stop his forward motion, which snapped something in his back and dropped him to his knees like he'd been shot. He went from his knees to his side and rolled over, motionless, moaning.

"Son of a bitch," Joseph said, though he was addressing his back, not the prick who lay beside him with his foot in the air.

"Fucking asshole," the guy said.

"I can't move," Joseph said.

"Good," said the prick. "I'm going to kick your ass."

He sounded so serious, Joseph laughed. He pictured the man standing on one leg, kicking and hopping on the other, like the knight in that Monty Python movie Melissa loved. He laughed

knocked him on his back. Then the guy lifted a block over his head and aimed for Joe's skull. He imagined Mei and his boys finding him dead, eyes open, an image that would chase them through their lives. Then the guy grimaced, dropped the block, collapsed to his knees, and rolled to his back, three feet from where Joe lay. He wasn't moving. Just moaning. Joe had left his phone inside but saw no urgent need to crawl toward it now because the big man was down.

"Son of a bitch," the guy said.

Joe's foot felt better from his back, leg raised, but it still throbbed.

"Fucking asshole," Joe said.

"I can't move," the guy said.

"Good," Joe said. "I'm going to kick your ass." And the guy started laughing.

Joe heard a history of ridicule that came from his older brother who had bullied him, from a bigger classmate who made him eat playground dirt, from so hard it made his back hurt, so he stopped laughing and moaned.

"I need a doctor," Joseph said.

The guy laughed, like Joseph deserved his pain, that he had dug his grave and must lie in it while the prick watched, laughing. Another in a long line of people who said punishment was good. Maybe they were right. Maybe if he ended up sharing a cell with his father, they could talk about it. Then he'd write long letters to Melissa, asking for forgiveness while staring at his cinderblock walls.

"You should call the cops," Joseph said.

"Good idea." But the guy didn't move. He kept his foot in the air. Joseph wondered if Melissa had made it to her mother's, if she'd try to call while he was in jail. He wondered if he'd ever work again, whether he'd qualify for disability.

"I left my phone inside."

"Use mine." He pulled it from his back pocket

motorists who mocked his spandex.

"I need a doctor," the guy said.

Joe said, "Ha." Not a laugh so much as a recognition of the absurd moment he found himself in, lying on his back next to a man who'd tried to murder him, who, according to his Hippocratic oath he'd have to treat if the guy was dying. Would he revive the guy just so the guy could try to kill him? Could this be the story he told Mei—how he chose to help a Neanderthal? Wouldn't she like that?

"Call the cops," the asshole said.

"Good idea," Joe said. But he didn't move. He needed a doctor too. He needed a cast, a boot, more Hydrocodone. If he had his phone, he'd call an ambulance. Maybe two. No, not two. That would be a waste of resources. They'd ride together.

"I left my phone inside," Joe said.

"Use mine." He scooted it across the ground toward Joe.

and pushed it toward him, moaning.

He looked at the sky. If rock-bottom meant landing in a spot where you couldn't sink further and you were looking up, wasn't that a start? Except he *could* sink further, without Melissa, without work. With a hurt back that would get worse. The dude wasn't reaching for the phone. They said nothing for a while, lying side by side like a long-married couple after an exhausting fight.

Joseph said, "What's wrong with rich pricks like you who can't be happy in places like this?"

"Good question. What's wrong with pricks like you who want to kill people?"

"Not all pricks. Just pricks like you."

They lay there awhile, saying nothing. A family of buzzards circled.

"Tell you the truth," the guy said. "I wish I worked outside like you."

"What are you, a god-damned doctor?"

"Seems to be a matter of opinion."

"Your bedside manner sucks," Joseph said.

He didn't reach for it. The sky was cloudless. Were Mei and the boys looking at it from their canoe, which is where he'd have them already if he were with them? He wondered when he'd be able to ride his bike again. What would he do in the meantime? Maybe try more of what he was doing now, being still, staring into the sky to trace the route of his failures?

The guy said, "What's wrong with rich pricks like you who can't be happy in places like this?"

"Good question. What's wrong with pricks like you who want to kill people?"

"Not all pricks. Just pricks like you."

They lie there awhile, saying nothing. A team of buzzards started circling.

Joe said, "To tell you the truth, I wish I worked outside like you."

"What're you, a god-damned doctor?"

"Seems a matter of opinion," Joe said.

"Your bedside manner sucks."

"Yeah, I get that sometimes."

The buzzards circled, dipped, and rose. The air was dissolving toward another day of intense heat people could blame for bad behavior. If he could find the words to make Melissa see him now—*if* she listened long enough—to make her understand how oddly comfortable he felt to be so powerless, how eager to surrender every desire except the one to make her happy, would she allow him another chance? He imagined walking with her and their child beside the river some sunny fall morning, relishing the soft air and bright leaves, greeting strangers and being greeted in return, stepping aside to share space when needed, to say *hey, look up, be alive.*

"Yeah, I get that sometimes," Joe said.

The buzzards glided in graceful circles, ascending, descending, drifting. The sun was burning off the morning coolness, moving toward another day of record-setting heat that would turn people angry. If he gave Mei enough time to get to a place where she agreed to listen; if he could find the words that matched the truth of how it felt so good right now to feel so small, would she say, at least, *we'll see?* He pictured a fall morning when he and she and the boys would be biking beside the river in the soft sun, crunching leaves, slowing to share a greeting with everyone they passed, to say *hey, good morning, pardon me please, no one today is dying.*

<h1 style="text-align:center">Coming or Going?</h1>

My father's heart stopped on a Friday in early August, while I was busy preparing to move away from him. Three days later, he called to tell me all about it. At that moment, I was busy buying beer, on a break from loading boxes into the moving truck. Maria and I were moving 1,400 miles from the Florida swamplands where my father's family had lived two hundred years. She'd landed a good job in Wisconsin, and I was going with her, hoping to land one too. We worried about leaving the only place we'd known and worried about loved ones whose hearts might stop, but her job meant we were supposed to worry less.

Had I known earlier that my father's heart had stopped, I would've said I'm sorry sooner. The cashier said the beer would be $5.02, but all I had were five wrinkled ones and no wallet where a credit card would be. I dug into my empty pockets and waited for her to act charitably, but she made no move.

If I had taken the time to take one of his earlier calls, I would've known sooner that his heart had stopped, but I didn't take his call until I took a break from packing. The cashier leaned against her counter and looked into my eyes for two pennies, but I was empty. I knew it was rude to be on the phone in the checkout line, but I'd figured on a fast and painless transaction, and I couldn't imagine a time when I'd have more time to talk to my father.

His voice sounded like his heart was beating fine.

I stared back into the cashier's eyes for two pennies. She was empty too.

He said, "You should have heard my voice three days ago."

Both of her eyes were giving me the stink eye.

When I told him, three months earlier, that we were moving way up north, he called me a one-way prodigal. I wondered whether the cashier was—to use a phrase my father liked to use—*devoid of consideration*. He called me a blue-coat Yankee. Maybe she didn't like my looks; sensed that *I* was the one devoid of consideration. He called me a lost spirit drifting. I kept one hand on my beer. He'd been afraid of dying alone in a dirty apartment surrounded by senior citizens in dirty apartments just like his. The cashier stood her ground. He was afraid his heart would burst before we made amends. I dug inside my empty pockets to show her I was trying. I'm my father's first and only, his last loved one.

An old lady behind me unsnapped her change purse and handed me two pennies. I thanked her and looked deeply into her eyes and wondered whether she was my dead grandmother come back to remind me what was important and what was not. She looked away, which meant she wasn't.

"Come see me," my father said into my phone. He lived thirty miles away, which may as well be 1,400 miles, he said, based on the number of times I'd seen him lately.

"Wish I could," I said. I explained how the house here and the house there had to close before the close of business in two days, minus an hour for the time difference, and we still had the beds to load and the carpet to clean before we could leave at the break of day.

"Well," he said.

I was in my car now, headed toward my U-Haul. The car with 180,000 miles on it that Maria would drive while

I followed in the U-Haul. I asked him to explain how his heart had stopped. There was no traffic.

It stopped while he was sleeping in a sleep study lab, he said, then some low-level intern administered a karate chop, at which point he woke and called the intern a dirty name. Just his luck, he said, that he'd have to die more slowly and painfully now, unrested, with no one around to pull a sheet over his long toenails before his body would be found.

"I'm sorry," I said.

The sleep scholars had hoped to diagnose the abnormality that made him wake up tired. Then sometime in the night a sensor caught him sleeping like a dead man, so the head sleep-nurse called the karate-chopping intern who had been sleeping peacefully in his office; therefore, the results were inconclusive. I said I was heavily sleep-deprived myself, and wouldn't sleep again that night because the walls were lined with boxes our sore backs had to lift and carry to the U-Haul I'd drive 1,400 miles over two days while dealing with three cats and their respective litter boxes that would share a motel room with us at the end of the first day's drive somewhere in the middle of an Illinois cornfield before we woke early and drove the rest of the way in order to get to the too-expensive house we'd bought on our first trip two months ago.

"Wish I could help you," he said.

I backed our car into the driveway so Maria could head out easily.

"We have too much stuff," I said.

"Just wait until my heart stops for good and I go to sleep for sure. Then you'll have too much stuff."

I told him the closing of the new house had to happen sooner than we'd anticipated, which was throwing off the timing of everything.

"You always had bad timing," he said. Which was true.

I opened a beer while I sat in the car and told my father that all the houses we didn't buy were looking better now.

The home inspector hired by the agent eager to sell us a house said the leaking basement was in great shape for a basement built in 1891. My father said all the nurses congratulated the intern for his perfect karate chop. The home inspector of our new house hired by the agent eager to sell us a house knocked his fist against the basement walls and said this was a house he'd buy in a heartbeat if he was buying a brand new house built in 1891. Then they told my father to get some rest. The home inspector stomped our new old floors to inspect their sturdiness. My father said he woke most mornings in pools of sweat, too tired to stand a shower. The home inspector said, "This floor won't let you down." Apnea was suspected, for which a mask and machine were prescribed. The narrow stairs of the new home were split-level, and the short ceilings were too severely sloped to allow the safe passage of a mattress made for two.

Restless leg syndrome was an accomplice, for which home remedies were recommended. But a mattress could be squeezed through an upstairs window, if one had a long-enough rope, and if one had learned what one should have learned long ago in the way of tying knots that could easily be untied, which I'd never learned. Placing bars of soap in the bed beneath the feet, for example, was a recommended home remedy, but the soap kept slipping, my father said.

The window would hold a bed. In his sleep, my father ran after his regrets, then woke where he started, sweating. The floor would hold a crying woman.

My father said, "Moving is stressful."

The walls were lined with boxes of books taped shut, stacked on boxes of clocks locked up. I didn't know what time it was.

I did not say, "Dad, do you remember thirty years ago when you took me to a zoo and sat me on your knee and asked me whether I knew if I was coming or going?"

He asked whether we might come and go again at Christmas.

I said I couldn't say.

"Just remember I'm always in your corner," he said. "Until I'm not."

I told him I'd take time to call while I was on the road driving away from him.

"Take time," he said.

All night that night while we loaded boxes and cleaned the carpet, the basketball across the street said *bounce*. We pulled the chord on the vacuum at 4 a.m., then I followed the bouncing ball into the shower and started laughing. My back was sick. I'd never lifted so much so fast with still so far to go, and when I stepped into the shower, I was struck with an attack of laughing the water seemed to cause. I couldn't otherwise see the source. Maria, concerned, stepped into the shower and caught the laughter too. She said, "Why are we laughing?" I told her I'd tell her later, but I never did.

We slept for an hour with open windows, but the bouncing ball came in. It said *bounce, bounce, bounce-bounce, breathe. Bounce, bounce, bounce-bounce, breathe.* An hour of sleep was like strange labor. I dreamed of a heart-shaped ball that hit the pavement and said *splat.* We woke in the dark and started driving. Somewhere in the middle of an ocean-sized cornfield in the middle of Illinois, where trees were absent to make more corn, I recalled a piece of a dream from my hour of sleep—my father's nurse had called to tell me I should come at once.

I called my father to make sure the nurse was full of shit.

He didn't answer. Then he did. He sounded like I woke him.

"Did I wake you?"

"No," he said. "I had to get up to answer the phone."

"Are you home?"

"Where else?"

"The hospital? The morgue?"

"Let me check," he said.

He paused. I drove the U-Haul one-handed down the interstate through the corn, waiting for children from a horror movie to emerge with scythes and sickles.

"Must be the morgue," he said. "Where are *you*?"

I told him.

"I hope you find what you're looking for," he said.

I paused. I looked ahead, toward Maria, who was moving north.

"I'm proud of you," he said. "You're my only child who's brave enough to leave his poor ol' Daddy and go so far from home in search of something good."

"I'm your *only* child."

"That's what I said. You get everything. Shouldn't be much longer."

"You sound sleepy."

"I haven't slept too well for thirty years. Since about the time you were born."

"I'm sorry," I said. Because I was.

"Do good. Work hard. Try to get above your raisin'."

"My raisin?"

"Your raisin'. Some tell you not to, but I say you ought to."

I followed Maria through the corn, big ball of fire sinking on the left, fat moon rising on the right. Hungry-eyed children stepped from the corn with scythes and sickles.

"It's nice here," I said.

"Here too," he said. "Call me when you land."

"I'll call you when I land."

"Good night and good luck," he said.

"Are those your final words?"

"Call me later. I'll try to do better."

I called him later. It was the following day, when the moving truck was empty. My back was sick, and I didn't know where I was.

He said, "Do you think you could come and go again once more, right now?"

"I'm on the way," I said.

He said, "I'm sorry."

Hospitality Lessons for Survivors

Dear Mysterious Light Source,

I'm ninety-four-years-old and shouldn't be in charge of correspondence, but who the fuck else is going to explain our behavior and ask for forgiveness? We'd heard stories over the years that you would appear one day out of the blue, but we'd stopped looking up long ago amidst all the dark news that had made us so weary for so long. But then came that Saturday night, July 3rd, at 11:03 p.m. when you came flooding into my bedroom like the moon had stepped through my window. We were given a chance to save ourselves. We blew it. I played a role in that, but I have my excuses like everyone. Could we have a do-over? Do you know English?

Times were tough, as the old-timers used to say, then things got worse. The last wave of sickness came through and food got scarce. I ate cheaply, for one, so I was lucky, even if I could barely stomach the frozen fish dinners that got delivered every Saturday if they weren't stolen from my doorstep first. A third of us were dead and another third were dying inside the local college, which had been converted into a hospice facility. I knew by the quality of your light that you intended to save us. I walked outside in my pajamas, phone in hand, and saw all my neighbors looking skyward too, like me. I called Mayor Bobbie.

"Of course, I see it," she said.

We'd known each other in high school when we were cheerleaders and stayed best friends for three years until Bobbie—well, that's another story, but then I went to college and stayed away for seventy years, then outlived my husband and child, and came home, finally, to find Bobbie in her third term as mayor, and we hugged, then she asked me to chair The Hospitality Committee, which I was happy to do, to be useful, to tell people we lived in a beautiful place worth visiting—worth returning to—even in the midst of pandemics and food shortages and countless killings over parking spaces, bumper stickers, and facial expressions.

Bobbie said everyone in her neighborhood, like everyone in mine, was standing in their front yards and in the street dressed in their underwear and nightgowns looking up into your light with their mouths hanging open. It saturated the whole town in a soft and majestic hue that hypnotized us into believing that everything would soon be okay.

"Looks like your new campaign is working," Bobbie said.

"It's a team effort," I said, which was true. Maybe you saw one of our spiffy digital billboards? Or our newly designed website featuring my photography?

"Now *everyone* will be descending on us," Bobbie said. "The media, scientists, UFO-chasers, the President."

"The President?"

"Probably."

"How embarrassing," I said.

"Let's call an emergency meeting of your committee so we can plan a proper greeting."

Our Hospitality Committee went to City Hall at once, in pajamas and nightgowns, except for Mitch McDonald, the asshole, who never left his house without a suit and tie. Bobbie had the conference room lit up, and we all came in talking all at once.

Lars said, "I bet their arrival is meant to coincide with our 4th of July celebration."

"We canceled our 4th of July celebration, dummy," Jill said. It was true. Our fireworks budget had dried up, and we wanted to discourage crowds to reduce infections.

"I'm sick and tired of your constant negativity," Lars said.

"Let's decide how best to welcome our visitors," Bobbie said.

"That's easy," said Mitch McDonald, the pompous ass. Then he proposed, and the committee approved (7-2), that we call an event planner who could plan a proper greeting.

"I know just the person," Mitch said.

He meant his third wife, Elaine McDonald. His second wife was my sister (now dead), whom he was married to for ten years thirty years ago. I stopped liking him the moment she introduced me, and he winked at me with one of his reptile eyes.

"Conflict of interest," Doris Turnbull said. "Nepotism. Yet another contract awarded because of special connections that continue to privilege the rich and powerful."

"She does good work," Lars said. "I remember last year's balloon maker."

"She knows the best food trucks and beer vendors," Susan said.

"And beer vendors," Bill said.

"I just said beer vendors," Susan said.

"My daughter loved that giraffe-balloon she got," Lars said.

Mitch called Elaine, who called food truck owners, beer vendors, balloon-makers, photographers, the whole shebang. *Shebang* is an American word, first used by Civil War soldiers and the poet Walt Whitman, according to Google's dictionary, and also means "rustic dwelling" or "hut," but now means "everything." A dictionary is a source that supplies definitions for words. Google is a computer program that provides information unrelated to the human soul. A human soul was the invisible essence (from the Greek, meaning "to breathe") "that comprised the mental abilities of a living being: reason, character, feeling, consciousness, memory, perception, thinking, etc." (Wikipedia, via Google). Some say souls live forever, some say souls don't exist. My grandmother called me "a lost soul forever drifting."

"Our next priority," Mitch said, "should be ticket sales. Imagine the revenue we'll generate by selling eighty thousand tickets at $5k per seat."

"Season ticketholders should get free access," Ron Zinker said.

"You're saying that because *you're* a season ticketholder," Jill said.

"I inherited them fair and square," Ron said.

"Listen," Lars said. "I have yet to hear anyone express the very real possibility that this strange light is coming from a dangerous source, such as a well-organized team of celebrities who intend to harm our children."

"Listen," Bob Evans said. "There's a liability risk here. Five thousand dollars per seat could get us sued for price-gouging."

"Listen," Lars continued. "An entire fleet of these things could be right behind this one."

Mitch McDonald, the reptile, said, "The free market creates a demand we're obliged to satisfy. This is a golden opportunity."

"We should build a protective space wall," Lars said. "We could convert the college into a space-wall plant. Supply chains would spring up everywhere, making space-wall parts."

Bobbie got quiet. She'd gone to the window to look out. She was mesmerized. Everyone else remained seated ten feet apart at the long table.

"With revenue from $5k per seat," said Mitch, "we could pay a space-wall manufacturer to establish a base that would create thousands of low-paying jobs for the unemployed, who increasingly rely on handouts."

"What we need is a bigger jail," Bill said.

"Remember when we had schools?" Doris said.

"I'm tired of your nostalgia," Lars said. "We have a clear and present danger."

"It's a liability risk," Bob said again.

Bobbie turned from the window, looking radiant. "Maria?"

Everyone looked at me, waiting for my opinion. I did not pause.

I said, "We should go right this second to stand beneath the light and smile and wave and show that we're friendly and invite them down for an area tour."

Mitch said, "We might avoid liability risks if we charged $2k per seat." In the form of a motion, he proposed, and the committee approved (7-2), that we sell tickets for $2,000.

"Including a commemorative knickknack," Herman said.

"Like what?" Jill said.

They argued over knickknacks: cups, pennants, hats, keychains.

"*I* know," Bruce said. Then he proposed, and the committee agreed (7-2) on digging out the boxes of t-shirts we'd ordered long-ago that said, "Welcome to God's Country," printed inside an image of our state's shape.

"Listen," Bobbie said. "I agree with Maria that we should proceed immediately to the light before it's too late."

"*Listen*," Lars said, in a mocking tone. "We should mobilize the National Guard, but we need the Governor's go-ahead."

"Has anyone called the Governor?" Jill said.

"Where *are* those t-shirts?" Lillian Rose said. "We could all wear one."

"Stadium's locked," Bob said.

"My brother-in-law has a key," said Mitch, the fucker. "But listen—"

"Bad idea," Lars said.

"Listen," Lillian said. "We can't greet them without a gift."

Everyone talked at once. Hell broke loose. There's a phrase you won't find in your guidebook. Hell is a place most of us are taught about as children—maybe you've heard stories. It's where "bad souls" are said to spend eternity being punished for earthly sins. Some (like Mitch McDonald) are said to have a special seat reserved there. Some hope others will rot there. And it's hot, allegedly, worse than Death Valley, CA.

Bill Schmidt crawled on the table, stood, raised his arms, shouted, "People, please!"

We grew quiet. Bill said, "I think we should greet them with…*a song.*" He spread his arms wide, proud of himself. He had once managed the community theatre and had starred in many musicals, but not for a very long time. "Music," he explained, "is the universal language. A song will reveal who we are. As a people," he clarified.

We paused.

"Depends on the song," Bruce said.

"It would have to be some kind of anthem of national significance," Mitch said.

"The Battle Hymn of the Republic," Bruce said.

"Amazing Grace is nice," Lillian said.

"John Phillips Sousa," said Joe J. Weiskopf.

"That's not a song," Jill said.

"*Philip,*" said Lars. "There's no S in Phillips, dumbfuck."

"I have a solution," said Mitch, the prick. He stood. Buttoned his suit coat. Then started singing. He was ninety-five-years-old, and his terrible and shaky singing voice didn't stop him from being loud. It was probably the highlight of his career—something he'd been wanting to do forever. Doris Turnbull made a face and pushed her fingers into her ears. It *was* awful. He kept going. He was *proud to be an American,* he sang. This was a song recorded by Lee Greenwood, as played at the 1984 Republican National Convention—a silly week-long series of propagandistic charades. This is when our leader at that time, Ron Reagan (former movie actor/celebrity and anti-communist crusader of the 1950s) ventured way out on a limb to proclaim that he himself was a proud American. Everyone went apeshit over that song, felt a zealous fervor that topped the fervor of the 1980 convention when the Reaganites played "Born in the U.S.A." (without permission of the author, Bruce Springsteen, to his great shame) because those were the only words they understood, words enough for an entire platform, no matter that the song was inspired by all the sorrow that came from so many Vietnamese and American deaths during the Vietnam War (1963-1973) that kept escalating while our leaders faced the cameras and repeatedly lied to us about how well the war was going.

McDonald kept singing. *He'd proudly stand up and defend her still today*, he sang. Doris went to the restroom and returned looking pale while McDonald moved to his big finish. He knew all the words, the idiot. When he finished, he sat, waiting for applause. There was none.

Doris announced that the song, as well as Mr. McDonald's rendition of it, had made her physically ill. "I have never vomited so forcefully," she declared.

"Ms. Turnbull," McDonald said, "I wonder if your diet might benefit from more moral fiber and less (sic) donuts."

Doris said, "Let the record re-reflect that Mr. McDonald is a biscuit-fucker."

McDonald denied the charge (despite a leaked photo), claiming a gluten allergy.

"Mrs. Turnbull," he said. "Though this slanderous assault against my character continues unabated, I will go on the record to say I would much prefer achieving intimacy with a cold biscuit than with the likes of someone as un-American as yourself."

Here followed a tense moment of silence. An important moment. We could have used the moment to save ourselves.

We could've taken a breath, regrouped, rebooted, relinquished egos.

Doris approached Mitch, stared him in his cold eyes, then snatched his toupee from his head and tossed it to the center of the table, where it lay like a dead squirrel. A toupee is a fake piece of hair some people tape to their heads to hide baldness. In the end, this is what killed us. If you are as hairless as many of our movies have depicted you, maybe it means you're more evolved than we. Isn't it easier to look each other in the eye and see what's in there if you're not distracted by someone's hair, or with thoughts of how your own hair compares? I've survived three bouts of cancer (breast, lung, breast), and can tell you that people were always kindest when I was bald. It has been reported that our national leader spends three hours each morning having his hair prepped, during which time he looks for himself on television.

Another moment of silence followed while we stared at the dead toupee. We could have used this second moment to reflect on our first failed moment. To his credit, McDonald rose from his seat, again buttoned his coat (making no mention of his baldness) and mentioned something about the necessity, "Yay, the urgency," he cried, "at this late hour, to reclaim our collective civility for the sake of our common survival." He paused to let this sink in.

Someone threw a shoe at him.

It was me. The song was bad enough, but when he said this last thing, he winked at me. After he winked, he kept talking, clearly headed toward a filibuster, which I could not allow. I suspect you have no need for this word, "filibuster." It means winning a point by talking until your colleagues' corpses have begun to rot.

Within seconds, hell proper emerged—my colleagues tossed water into each other's faces. They kicked each other's shins. Stabbed each other with pencils, pulled hair, freeing three other toupees and one wig. Canes were parried and riposted, wheelchairs toppled, all amid some of most horrid flatulence I've endured. Dick Gustafson, who had yet to say a word, opened his briefcase and removed the grenade his great-grandfather had given him the Christmas little Dick was a first grader being bullied for wearing a camouflaged Army helmet to school on account of his soft skull. Everyone had heard the story, but little Dick told it again, slowly, even as the battle royal ensued and no one made any effort to hear him. Then he pulled the pin and dropped the grenade between his feet.

Inside the smoky room, amidst the chaos, I started choking whoever I could get my hands on. Turns out the throat belonged to Mitch McDonald, who was already dead. I had a dark thought I'm not proud of: if only I'd acted sooner, *I* could have killed him. I ripped a cane from the cold hands of an elder statesman (Lars Hanson, as it turned out) who had whacked me in the lower torso, and I thrust the tip of the cane into his chest, which, surprise to me, stuck into his doughy flesh. He raised his eyes to the ceiling and sobbed and called out for his long-dead mother, a town founder. It was embarrassing.

Needless to say.

When the meeting adjourned, about midnight, all of us—except Mitch, Lars, and Dick—limped outside, me with one bare foot. Right away, in unison, we looked skyward. You were gone, of course. We stood still a second, stared at a distant and lonely star, wishing, but it was pointless. No one said anything. We lowered our heads and walked away in different directions. I removed my shoe and carried it through the dark and empty streets until I reached my bed again, then slept for two days, full of regret and shame.

A month later, groceries grew more scarce. Doris Turnbull died. Everyone else on the committee was sick. Except

Bobbie. Bobbie, who was alone like me, suggested we live together, pool our resources. She apologized for stealing my boyfriend in eleventh grade, and I forgave her. Her term was up in November, and she tried to persuade me to run in her place, using the same slogan she used, which was the same one her predecessor used, which was: "It's time for a change." We laughed all night at this. Do you know the phenomenon of human laughter? It's a reflex triggered when madness collides with truth.

But as my grandmother used to say, "Sometimes, it ain't funny."

Last Wednesday, the day after it was announced that football season had been canceled, someone blew up the stadium, which was full of dead people—even all the seats— because the college classrooms and offices and dorm rooms were already full. Some were quick to blame a group of fans from a rival team in a nearby state. There's no evidence, but blaming them keeps us from looking too closely at ourselves, which is a comfort.

This is the first letter I've written since I went away for college and got so homesick. I wrote letters every day back then, telling my mom how much I wanted to come home. It'll be my last letter, too, which makes me feel kind of, well, kind of poetic I guess. You ever had a near-death mishap in your spaceship and plummet twenty-thousand feet in three seconds and start making promises that you'll make your short life matter and find ways to help others, then on the way home, you get into a traffic jam while listening to the news and that feeling flies away as fast as you raise your middle finger at the speeding asshole with the wrong bumper sticker? That's how I feel now that I'm ninety-five-years-old.

On behalf of our entire species, I apologize for scaring you off. I shouldn't have thrown my shoe. It turns out Mitch was right, the bastard. We had a chance to reclaim civility, and I blew it. I'm trying to forgive myself.

Today, Saturday, Bobbie and I didn't get a grocery delivery. We sat in my back yard beneath my two white cedars and listened to music. We discussed what singer's voice might soothe us best—what voice might lure you back. We agreed to start with Ray Charles. We played his version of "America the Beautiful." I'm not crazy about the schmaltzy sea to shining sea stuff, but if there's someone that would make you turn around, a voice to make you hear the longing and the hope and the immense pain of our failings and our desperate yearning to do better, it's Ray's voice. There's a prayer in Ray's voice. A prayer is a solemn request for help, an earnest hope or wish. Ray makes you see what a well-lit soul looks like. In the 1960s, he was banned from singing in the city of Atlanta because of his skin color, this in the same state where he was born. Still, he later recorded the best version of "Georgia on My Mind," which will make you want to go there just to see the moonlight through the pines.

Then we played Nina Simone's "Mississippi Goddamn." Such anguish and rage and grief even as Nina makes you tap your foot. I said, "Bobbie, get your ass up and let's dance." So she did, and I did and it made our minds go quiet for a while. Then she started coughing, and we hugged a good long while without needing to say anything. Then we sat still and played Nina's "Feeling Good." Bobbie's cough grew worse. But Nina put a spell on us, made us believe we were young and beautiful. We watched the sky, thinking you might appear again, but neither of us said what we were thinking.

Then Bobbie said, "Oh no!"

"What now?" I said.

She pointed out that I had started coughing too, which I hadn't noticed.

"You know," I said, "I'm really tired of your negativity." And we laughed. We laughed and coughed and laughed and coughed until we both fell out of our chairs. I landed on my side, pen in hand, notebook still beneath it.

"Guess what?" I said.

"What now?" she said.

"I think I broke a hip."

And she laughed and coughed and laughed then coughed. She said, "You're killing me. I'm dying over here."

I said, "Me too."

We said, "Ahhhh."

She said, "If they come back and can't find us, tell them to look in the freezer."

"How are we going to get into the freezer?" I said.

"Not for us, dummy. For the fish."

"Right." There's a few frozen tilapia in there you'd like. One of our slogans was, "You haven't been to God's Country 'till the tilapia are swimming in your belly."

Blossoms were on the trees. A gentle breeze drifted by. Dragonflies danced in the sun. Butterflies—yes, *butterflies*—were having fun. We waited to see what the new dawn said. It would be a new day. A bold day.

Acknowledgments

I'm grateful to the editors of journals where some of these stories first appeared: "What Doesn't Kills Us Makes us Stranger" (as "What Kills Us") in *Carolina Quarterly*; "Reunions, Atrocious Manners, the Atlanta Airport" in *South Carolina Review*; "The Enormous Typewriter" in *Literal Latte*; "Coming or Going?" in *8142 Review*; "Music Appreciation for Dead People," *Wisconsin People & Ideas*, published as the 2023 fiction prize-winner, judged by Debra Monroe; "Please Pass the Flotsam" in *Florida Review*; "Hospitality Lessons for Survivors" as ("See You Soon") and "Love Song for the Headless" in *Cutleaf Journal*, where Keith Pilapil Lesmeister made each better.

I'm grateful to early readers, friends, supporters, and sympathizers who donated encouragement, advice, and friendship. Jerry Saviano, for example, who inhabited creative writing classrooms with me thirty-five(ish) years ago, where we absorbed insight and encouragement from a young professor named Robin Hemley, who somehow took us seriously. And Joseph Bathanti, who, for thirty years, has inspired me as a writer who writes and a human who helps. Thanks also to Bob L. Powell, Roxanne Newton, Brian Turner, Patrick Gilsenan, Andrea Selser, Ehud Havezelet, Tracey Daugherty, the Terrell & Jean Beck Sanctuary for Wayward Southerners, Robert L. Treu, William Stobb, David Krump, Susan

Crutchfield, Kelly Sultzbach, BJ Hollars, Jon Crane, Elder Olson, Otis Redding, and Pearl Street Books. Thanks also to good-spirited literary citizens like George Singleton for his body of excellent work and for answering a stranger's longwinded fan letter/email inside of an hour with a "Yes!" followed by news of distant weather. Thanks to Lori Ostlund for writing *me* a kind email to say an early version of this book had been a finalist for the annual Flannery O'Connor Competition, and who then agreed to read a later version and write even kinder words. Thanks to Patricia Henley for a nice phone call. Big thanks to Dr. Ross Tangedal, Brett Hill, Eleanor Belcher, Kimberly Janesch, Sophie McPherson, Sam Bjork, Karlie Harpold, and the entire Cornerstone crew, as well as to those who support them as a valuable indie press.

Thanks to all the students I've been privileged to work with over so many years who have taught me how to talk and how to listen and how to appreciate so many stories from so many points of views, how to keep it real, how to keep laughing, learning and laughing again.

Thanks to Myrna and Clayton Jett, lovely and gracious in-laws who immediately invited me inside, then asked me to sit and stay awhile.

I'm grateful to my father, John Fred Cashion (deceased), the first reader of my first writings (in the form of letters), who said send more, and the stubborn hero of many stories already published and the resilient hero of many true stories to come.

I'm grateful to have grown up under the influence of my maternal grandparents, Alberta & Chunky Burgess and with much support from the Burgess Family Foundation for Prodigal Sons (*hey Wezee!*). And to all other aunts, uncles, and cousins from all sides, here, there, yon, & gone, (even Greg G., who *might* be reading this)—I'm grateful for your goodnesses.

To my mother: thanks for enduring the birth pains. And thanks for enduring every subsequent pain I caused after that. Thanks for the typewriter you somehow saw fit to bestow upon me the Christmas I turned ten (though I certainly never asked for such a toy), which inspired me to bang out my earliest and sloppiest literature (in the form of letters). Thanks for refusing to scold me in front of Sister Mary Joan, who pointed in horror at the desktop I'd vandalized with a lead-drawn full-scale military battle scene (in miniature) I devoted my entire fourth grade career to developing (there were planes, trenches, mountains, men near and far killing and dying in shadows). Thanks for saying, "Wow! That's impressive." Thanks for then supplying me with expensive canvases you stretched and staple-gunned to wood so I could make more proper messes. Thanks for dancing down the hall (if dancing is the word) while I played the drumset you allowed in the center of the living room. Through all the lean years of single motherhood, and through all the many times I tested your grace, and through all the many times I reported my failures, thanks for remaining my champion.

Heather Jett. Thank you for being more alive than any other entity in this galaxy or the next and for being my best teacher in all the ways of what it means to becoming a better man. My lucky life is a gift from you.

MATT CASHION is the author of *Our 13th Divorce* (2017), *Last Words of the Holy Ghost* (2015), and *How the Sun Shines on Noise* (2005). Winner of the Katherine Anne Porter Prize, the Edna Ferber Fiction Award, and the Zona Gale Award for Short Fiction, he lives in La Crosse, Wisconsin.

www.ingramcontent.com/pod-product-compliance
Lightning Source LLC
Chambersburg PA
CBHW020032310726
48970CB00007B/2230